Charm School

HEDGEWITCH FOR HIRE – BOOK 12

CHRISTINE POPE

CHARM SCHOOL

ISBN: 978-1-946435-75-0

Published by Dark Valentine Press

Cover design by Lou Harper

Ebook formatting by Indie Author Services

Chapter 1

HEY, LITTLE SISTER

"YOU'LL NEED TO MAKE A DECISION SOON," my husband Calvin said. His tone was very gentle, but the expression in the dark eyes that met mine was almost stern, as though he knew he'd coddled me long enough...but time had finally run out.

Didn't I know it. The first of March had come and gone several days ago, and that meant this baby would be here in two weeks whether or not I'd solved the conundrum of who should run my shop while I was on maternity leave.

"What decision is left?" I returned, knowing I sounded bitter...even as I also had to acknowledge that the current situation was at least partly my fault. True, no one could have foreseen that the first person I'd hired, Melanie Knowles, would turn out to be a murderer and a liar, but still, the analysis paralysis that had followed those terrible revelations was definitely all on me. The rational side of my nature would probably have been forced to admit that the odds of another candidate for the job being equally duplicitous were very low, and yet, even though I'd dutifully relisted the job on Craigslist and asked everyone I knew in Globe to spread the word, the couple of people I'd interviewed just hadn't felt right to me.

I still believed I was offering an excellent compensation package, one that included insurance and paid days off, but it seemed not as many people were eager to relocate to a small town of only around seven thousand residents as all those Hallmark holiday movies might have led me to believe.

Calvin let out a breath. Not quite a sigh, because he knew better, but still, I could tell even his almost limitless patience had worn thin.

"People will understand if you have to close for a while," he said. "It's not forever. And it's not as if we have to depend on the income from the store."

No, we didn't. His salary as chief of the San Ramon tribal police would have been enough on its own to manage our day-to-day expenses, but I was also sitting on a huge pile of money in various investments, thanks to the multimillion-dollar inheritance I'd received from Lucien Dumond, my one-time nemesis and former head of GLANG—aka, the Greater Los Angeles Necromancers' Guild.

Mostly I believed that he'd left me the money as a way of flipping the bird to his followers and his murderous younger brother, Eugene, but still, the money had made it so I—and, by extension, my husband—would never have to worry about our finances even if we were left with no other means of support.

All the same, I'd worked hard to make Once in a Blue Moon a fun and unique store, a place where locals and tourists alike could stop in to buy a crystal or a book on Bigfoot or a deck of Tarot cards, and the thought of leaving it shuttered for the next six months...or maybe longer...made me hurt deep inside. It hadn't been Lucien's money that had bought the shop and the accompanying apartment above it, but my own savings, helped by a modest windfall thanks to the California lottery back when I'd still been living in L.A. The apartment was long gone, now transformed into a design studio belonging to my friend Victoria Parrish, but I still felt far too connected to the building to just walk away for an indefinite period.

For the past few months, my friend Hazel Marr had been helping me out when she could, and I'd hired a girl named Olivia Barnes to come in afternoons and on Saturdays, but neither one of them was a long-term solution to my problem. Olivia was a senior in high school and had already been accepted at Arizona State University, so she would be gone after the end of July, and Hazel...well, Hazel was going to have her hands full in the very near future.

"Chuck and I didn't want to tell anyone until we were sure," she'd confided in me just a week earlier. "But everything's progressing well, and I'm due at the end of September."

Of course I'd had to hug her and congratulate her—and be thrilled that my best friend would have a child so close in age to Calvin's and mine. I'd almost immediately gotten misty at the thought of the two of them playing together...even as I realized that the off-and-on help Hazel had been able to provide these past few months wasn't anything I could depend on for the long term.

Which had made me redouble my efforts to find someone to run the store while I was on leave, even as I realized I probably was going to strike out yet again.

And that had led to Calvin and me sitting there at the dining room table, ignoring our plates of spaghetti while he brought up the uncomfortable subject. Just as well, because even though I'd eaten heartily through most of my pregnancy, these past couple of weeks the baby had felt as though he—or she...we'd decided we wanted to be surprised—was pressing directly on my stomach, and invariably I'd feel full after taking only a few bites.

"Then I'll just have to close," I said. "Yes, I

could probably get Olivia and Hazel to keep things going for a few more months, but what would be the point? Especially since neither of them knows much about managing the inventory and keeping the books."

Calvin gave me a sympathetic nod. It was one thing to come in and assist customers and ring up purchases, and something else altogether to do all the finances and keep track of orders. I'd be the first to admit that I didn't much like that part of the business, either, but I'd always looked at it as a necessary evil while working in a place that otherwise was a labor of love. Neither Hazel nor Olivia viewed the store the same way I did, and I couldn't really expect them to. That was the whole reason why I'd wanted someone there full-time, someone who would care as much about the offerings in the latest catalog from Hay House as I did.

But because I hadn't been able to find anyone like that, better to shutter the place for the next six months and then see what happened. Calvin and I had already agreed that six months was the absolute minimum I would stay home before going back to work. Yes, we had an ample supply of eager and willing babysitters, thanks to his large and extended family—and also including my mother, who would be arriving in Globe the day after tomorrow with her husband Tom so they'd be here just in case the baby came early—but still, I wanted to be home all that time so I wouldn't miss a single precious moment with Calvin's and my child.

Whether I'd feel all right about going back to work after just six months was another story. It was entirely possible that the moment would come and I'd feel as though it would be better to be a stay-at-home mother for the foreseeable future.

But that day was still many months away. Right now, I needed to focus on the next few weeks...or maybe just days. After all, babies didn't always arrive when you expected them to.

"Okay," I said, knowing how heavy my voice sounded, "I'll start working on closing things down, and I'll let everyone know this is the last week Once in a Blue Moon will be open for quite a while."

Josie Woodrow stared at me, aghast. The weather had warmed up just enough that she'd abandoned the wool blazers she'd worn during the winter and now instead had on one that was heavy linen in a shocking pink shade that clashed wildly with her bright red hair. "You're really going to close?"

"I don't have much choice," I said sadly. That conversation with Calvin had taken place on Sunday night, so at least I had a full week to be here at the shop and say my goodbyes to everyone. And because it was a Monday morning, I was there alone, since Olivia wouldn't be in until three-thirty and Hazel only came to help out on Fridays and Saturdays. "I haven't been able to find anyone to fill the position, and Hazel is going to have much better things to do with her time."

Since Josie also knew about Hazel and Chuck's impending bundle of joy, she gave a sage nod, her light blue eyes still troubled. "I just can't believe you couldn't find anyone to take the job. You made it very attractive."

Yes, I did. However, I wouldn't mention to Josie that it was most likely a reluctance to relocate to such a small town that had severely cut down my applicant pool. She was a native of Globe, and, as its number-one real estate agent—and mayor—she never wanted to hear anything negative about the only place she'd ever called home.

While I loved living here and didn't regret for a second my impulsive decision to buy property in the small Arizona town and get the hell out of Los Angeles, I also had to admit Globe was just a wee bit lacking in amenities. The Super Walmart was the only game in town when it came to day-to-day shopping; otherwise, you had to drive a good hour and a half to get to Gilbert or the other southeast suburbs of Phoenix where you could visit the sorts of places I'd taken for granted when living in Southern California, like Trader Joe's or Costco or any other of a number of chain stores. True, shopping wasn't the only measure of the livability of a location, but it was still something most people needed to take into consideration when thinking about moving to a new town.

Also, with a population of just seven thousand people, Globe wasn't exactly a hotbed of social possibilities for someone in their twenties or thirties who might be looking for a long-term relationship. I'd gotten lucky in finding Calvin...and Hazel and Victoria had been equally lucky in meeting their husbands...and yet I had to admit to myself that not everyone would have the same kind of good fortune.

About all I could do was make a noncommittal sound in response to Josie's comment before adding, "But I'm going to try to make it fun for everyone—I'm going to make everything fifty percent off this week, which means it'll be easier for people to stock up on the things they need before I close the store."

This prospect—the idea had come to me while I was driving in to work—didn't seem to mollify Josie very much. One penciled auburn eyebrow lifted, and she said, "That may be fine in the short term, but people are still going to run out of supplies they're used to getting here at the shop. And what about Joyce?"

Joyce Lewis was married to Henry Lewis, the

chief of Globe's police force. He and I hadn't exactly seen eye to eye on a lot of things, to put it mildly...he wasn't enamored of having an amateur like me solve crimes on a regular basis...and yet Joyce and I got along very well, and I sold her wonderful candles in my store. Yes, she'd expanded her business to include shops in Gilbert and Queen Creek and even up in Payson, but I was still her biggest customer by far. Having Once in a Blue Moon closed indefinitely would for sure cause a hit to her bottom line.

"I'll make a big order with her before I close," I promised. "It's not as if the candles are going to go bad sitting in the stock room for a few months. So that should help a little."

Josie still didn't look entirely convinced, but she must have decided it wasn't fair to give me a guilt trip about the situation, not when I'd tried my best to find someone to manage the store for me. Instead, she gave a little sigh, one small enough that I could choose to ignore it, and said, "Well, I suppose that is something. Just let me know when you have some sale flyers made up—I can post one in the window of my office, and put another up on the bulletin board at City Hall."

I told her that would be wonderful, and she said goodbye a moment later and hurried out. While I'd never be an artist like Hazel, I'd gotten fairly proficient at using Canva and knew I'd be able to produce a variety of eye-catching sales materials that I could print out on the color laser printer in my office. No point in trying to get them professionally done, not when I was working on such a tight deadline.

Now filled with purpose, I reached under the counter to the shelf where I stored my laptop—a simple movement that had gotten more and more difficult over the past month—and booted it up. Monday mornings at the shop were always slow, and I figured I might as well take advantage of this free time while I could.

With any luck, business would get downright brisk once word got out that I was having the witchy equivalent of a fire sale.

Sure enough, after Josie dropped by to pick up the flyers I'd made for her and Hazel came over as well to help spread the word, the store was crowded with far more people than I could have reasonably expected to see on an early Monday afternoon. In fact, it was busy enough that I kind of wished Hazel had been able to stick around, since Olivia wouldn't be in for a few more hours.

"But I can't stay," Hazel told me after she came by to let me know she'd posted a flyer in the window of the Sundowner Gallery, a place down the street that sold a lot of her paintings, and added that she'd handed out the rest of them to people at Walmart when she stopped in to pick up a few things. Although I knew she was three months along, her pregnancy wasn't showing at all yet, and she looked remarkably like the woman I'd met three years earlier when I first came to town, tall and slim, with light brown hair and eyes that matched her name. "I have a doctor's appointment, and Chuck's meeting me there."

"It's fine," I assured her, even as I inwardly hoped it would be. So far, everyone had been very solicitous of my advanced pregnancy and hadn't asked me to clamber down off the padded stool where I sat most of the time when I was at the store and waddle over to help them locate a particular book or crystal. Well, if someone needed my personal assistance, they were just going to have to wait for as long as it took. "The last thing I expect is for you to skip seeing your doctor because of me. It'll be fine."

She sent me a relieved smile and hurried out, even as she promised to stop by the next morning and help out for a few hours. It was on the tip of my tongue to tell her that wasn't necessary, but then I reminded myself I could probably use all the help I could get this week. Besides, she was positively blooming and had already informed me that she hadn't experienced any morning sickness or anything that would prevent her from lending a hand for the next few days, so it wasn't as if I was imposing too much.

And after the next few days, her assistance wouldn't be necessary...not here at the shop, anyway. An only child, she didn't have a lot of experience with infants, and she'd already said she'd love to help out when my baby came along.

"I can be Auntie Hazel,' she'd said, and I'd been just fine with that idea. After all, I didn't have any siblings, either—well, except my half-brother and sister back in California, whom I'd never even met —so I thought it would be a great idea for the two of us to learn together. I'd have Calvin's mother Delia to lean on for advice...after raising five children and numerous grandchildren, there wasn't much about tending to infants that she didn't know...but still, I also really loved the idea of my best friend and I going on that kind of shared journey.

Despite how kind my customers were being about allowing me to remain seated on my stool, I couldn't quite keep my gaze from straying to the clock whenever I had a spare second. It seemed to be ticking along more slowly than usual, making it feel as if three-thirty would never get here. True, sometimes Olivia could make it in by three-fifteen, but a lot depended on how fast she could get off the school grounds and over to the store. Some people thought it was silly for her to come in and work for only two hours—the shop closed at five, but she stayed that extra half hour to tidy up and do any restocking that might be required—but I was paying her twenty-five bucks an hour, making it definitely worth her while.

To my relief, there was a small ebb in foot traffic at the shop a little before three o'clock, probably because people had to leave to pick up their kids at school. I let out a little sigh of relief after the last person went on their way, hoping inwardly that it would remain quiet until Olivia got here. At that point, I could continue working at the cash register while she helped anyone who might need immediate assistance locating a book or a particular kind of incense, and my stress level would go down quite a bit.

At about ten after three—I knew the exact time because I'd just sent another glance at the clock mounted on the wall behind the counter—the door to the shop opened and a woman...not much more than a girl, really, maybe around twenty-one or twenty-two...entered. I'd never seen her before, so I guessed she must be someone passing through town. We got more than our fair share of tourists, mostly people heading to Phoenix from Payson or vice versa, so it wasn't too unusual to spot a stranger in the shop, even though Monday afternoon wasn't exactly prime time for tourists and spring break wouldn't start for another few weeks at least, depending on the school involved.

"Can I help you?" I asked as she approached the counter.

Her gaze strayed to my obviously swollen midsection. No, I'd never gotten as big as some women did at this stage of their pregnancy, but it still must have been pretty obvious that I was about to pop any day now.

Then she looked back up at me. Her eyes were an unusual color, a pure dark gray without a hint of blue, and her long hair, just as sooty as mine, reached to the middle of her back. She wore a knee-length black dress and black boots, with a jean jacket over the ensemble as a nod to the weather outside, which was sunny but still a little chilly, hinting of spring but not quite there yet.

"Hi, Selena," the strange girl said. "I'm your sister Chloe."

Chapter 2

ALL THE WORLD

It was probably a good thing I was sitting on that stool, because I didn't have to worry about my knees giving way and depositing all eight-plus-months-pregnant of me on the shop floor. About all I could do was blink at this apparition and say, "I beg your pardon?"

She grinned. I wouldn't say we resembled one another too much despite the similarity in our hair color—my face was oval, while hers was heart-shaped, and she had the kind of skin that looked as if it tanned easily, while I was pale and tended to fry in the sun—but something about that flash of a smile did seem like mine, wide and friendly.

"I know it must be kind of a shock," she said. "But I finally was able to figure out where you were living, and I really wanted to meet you."

This time, I managed to reply, "How did you find me?"

Not even a blink. "I consulted the Tarot."

Most other people might have responded to such an admission with scorn. However, since I regularly read Tarot cards to help me with major life decisions, I didn't find anything too strange about her answer.

Or rather, it seemed natural enough to me that someone might use such a method for life guidance. What felt utterly crazy, though, was that this half-sister of mine might possess anything similar to my own gifts. While I'd never questioned where my intuition…or my ability to see auras, as unreliable as it often was…might have come from, now I had to wonder.

Was it possible that my talents had come from my absent father's side of the family, rather than some long-ago great-great maternal grandmother?

"I didn't think you would think that was weird," Chloe went on. "I mean, considering your store and everything."

She made a small wave toward the table that held what I called the "pocket crystals," the less expensive rock specimens that were the perfect size to ride along in your purse or be tucked under a pillow…or sit on an altar, the way I had a bunch of them displayed at home.

"Oh, I don't think it's weird," I said quickly. "I

suppose I was just surprised that you read the Tarot like I do."

"My dad says it runs in the family," Chloe returned. "Or at least, he heard from my grandmother that her grandmother supposedly had the Sight. He says he's not psychic at all, but it must have popped up in me."

She sounded entirely blithe about the situation. But then, if Chloe had been living with her powers for most of her life, then I supposed she was probably used to them by now, even though she looked as though she was about ten years younger than me and therefore barely out of her teens.

Because that was pretty much all I knew about my half-siblings. I knew that Chloe and her brother existed, that her brother was about eight years my junior and Chloe had followed a couple of years later. Jordan Fairfield—my biological father—had made it clear that, while he was willing to pay child support, he hadn't planned for me to be born and didn't want to be part of my life beyond making sure I was provided for. Early on, the realization that he'd basically cut me out of his life had hurt a lot, but as time had worn on and I'd gained some perspective, I'd decided it was better that way. Why try to force someone to love you when he viewed you as nothing more than a mistake?

But Jordan had gotten older and wiser after that time when he'd been drumming in a metal band, had gotten his degree in music, had ended up teaching school and having a family of his own. From time to time over the years, I'd wondered if I should try to reach out to my half-siblings, and something had always stopped me. Not my mother; she'd made her peace with the situation, and while she might have tried to gently let me know that we were all living our separate lives, she would never have outright forbidden me to make contact. Instead, I'd let it go.

However, it appeared that Chloe had no intention of doing the same thing.

"So...the Tarot told you where to find me," I said. "That's interesting, because the Tarot is kind of how I ended up in Globe in the first place."

My newfound half-sister beamed. She was a very pretty girl, with the kind of smile that made her light up from the inside. Because the only photo I'd ever seen of my biological father was a grainy snapshot someone had taken of him at the club where he'd been playing when he met my mother, I'd never had a very good impression of his looks, except that he might have been halfway handsome if it weren't for that ridiculous heavy-metal shag he'd been sporting.

Ah, the '90s.

So maybe Chloe took after him in looks, or maybe she favored her mother. Since I knew nothing about the woman, not even her name, I couldn't hazard a guess.

"That's exactly what led me here," Chloe said. "I mean, I turned twenty-one in February, and something about that birthday made me start thinking about things. Like, I graduated from college a semester early because of my AP credits and all that, but I wasn't sure what I wanted to do with my life. Then I remembered how my dad said once that you were a professional psychic, but everything I tried to look up on you was out of date, and your website was gone altogether."

"Yes, I took that down after I moved here," I said, a smile of my own tugging at my lips. Maybe some people would have been annoyed to have an unexpected sibling pop up like this out of the blue, but something about Chloe's enthusiasm was infectious.

She nodded, dark hair slipping over her shoulder. Like mine, it was straight and thick, although much longer than I'd ever worn it. "That was when I decided to consult the Tarot. The first card I pulled was The World."

Just as I had several years ago, scared to death that Lucien Dumond was after me and knowing I needed to get out of L.A. as fast as I could. The cards had led me to Globe back then...just as they had for Chloe now.

I tilted my head, indicating she should go on, so she continued.

"First I tried Googling your name and 'the world,' but that didn't pull up anything. And there are more Selena Marxes out there than I'd thought there would be, so I didn't find anything right away."

I'd learned that same thing several years earlier, so this particular piece of information didn't surprise me too much. "But then…."

Chloe's shoulders lifted. "I kept thinking about it, though, and I had a flash of inspiration. Like, I remembered that the world is a globe, so I looked up that word combined with your name. And bam—there was the link to your store's website. At first, I couldn't believe I'd been that lucky, but then I realized it was my intuition that had guided me here."

Again, since I was someone who generally heeded that same inner voice, I couldn't fault my half-sister for following her gut, even if doing so was the kind of following blind belief that a lot of people would have considered foolish at best.

"Does your father know you're here?" I asked.

Her shoulders lifted in a too-nonchalant shrug. "I'm an adult," she said. "I don't need to ask his permission."

Maybe not, but she seemed like a very young

twenty-one to me. At that age, I'd been on my own for several years.

But I reminded myself that comparisons were a waste of time and energy, so I put that somewhat judge-y thought aside.

Instead, I asked, "You're out on your own?"

Her slate-hued gaze slid away from mine. "Well, not exactly," she said after a long pause. "I mean, I kind of still live at home. But I pay rent. It's not like I'm sponging off my parents or anything."

The tone in her voice was just defensive enough that I knew I'd better leave it alone. "That's your business," I said lightly. "I suppose I just meant that it was a long way to drive without letting anyone know where you've gone."

At once, Chloe's expression lightened. "Oh, I told my mom," she said. "And she told me I just needed to be safe, which I was. Had my phone on the whole time, and didn't make eye contact with anyone when I stopped for gas. And see? I made it to Globe just fine."

"That you did," I replied. "And I have to say it's a very pleasant surprise to see you here. Do you have a place to stay lined up?"

Her pretty white teeth tugged at her lower lip, and then she said, "Not really. I guess I was kind of hoping I might crash at your place." Again, her gaze slid toward my rounded stomach. "But I suppose that's probably not a great idea."

I couldn't help smiling, even though I knew some people might have been annoyed by her assumption that it would be just fine to couch-surf at her previously unknown sister's house. Right then, I could only imagine Calvin's reaction if I brought Chloe home. Technically, we had the space to put her up, since we still had a spare room even after converting one of the extra bedrooms into a nursery, but I had a feeling he wouldn't be too thrilled to have a houseguest when our first child was ready to meet the world in less than two weeks.

No, I had something else in mind.

"My house is pretty far outside town," I said. "And while I know my husband Calvin would love to meet you, I have a better idea. A friend of mine has an Airbnb about five minutes from here, and I'm pretty sure it's available. Do you mind if I give her a quick call and make sure?"

"That would be great," Chloe replied. "The town looks kind of cute, so it would be fun to stay someplace where I could check things out."

"Then just give me a minute. You can go ahead and take a look around if you want."

She seemed amenable to that idea and headed toward the shelves that held my collection of Tarot cards for sale. Good timing, too, because the door opened right then, and a couple of customers came in. They went straight for the candles, though, and since it looked as if everyone was ready to browse in peace for a while, it seemed like the perfect opportunity for texting Hazel.

Hey, I just had an unexpected family member show up. Is your Airbnb available?

After I sent the message, I realized that Hazel might be in the middle of her doctor's appointment and wouldn't be able to respond right away. To my relief, though, her answer popped up only a moment later.

It's available. I have someone coming on the 21st, but that's a ways off.

Nearly three weeks from now. I could only hope that Chloe would have gotten her itch scratched by then and headed back to the San Fernando Valley, because I would definitely have my hands full by that point.

Perfect. Can you meet us there after 5:30?

I'll just put the key under the mat. It'll be easier.

Right, because I realized Hazel probably wouldn't want to hang around in Globe, waiting for me to get off work. No, I was sure she'd already planned to go home with Chuck to their ranch after her doctor's appointment.

That's fine. Thanks so much.

No problem. You can fill me in later.

And that meant she wanted to know who I was putting up in the Airbnb, which made perfect sense. Although I'd told Hazel that I had half-siblings out there in the world, I doubted she would ever imagine either of them was my unexpected guest. The only relatives who were truly part of my life were my mother and Tom, and since they owned a large Victorian mansion on the edge of town, it wasn't as if they had any need to crash in someone's Airbnb. True, there were Tom's kids and their spouses, but the mansion was big enough to hold all of them if necessary.

Luckily, though, none of that group had any desire to be present in Globe for the birth of my child. We managed to be civil to one another on the few occasions when we were forced to spend time together, but I had nothing in common with them and they had nothing in common with me and my husband, and I was more than happy to have them safely several hundred miles away the vast majority of the time. Tom himself was a different matter—I often wondered how such a wonderful man had managed to have such irritating children, and guessed they took after his ex-wife—but even he probably wasn't going to stay in Globe the entire time my mother planned to be here. Instead, he'd go back to SoCal as necessary if any important concerns came up regarding his plumbing supply business, then would return to Arizona once anything pressing had been handled.

Chloe came wandering back from the crystal

display, her gaze inquiring, and I said, "It's all settled—Hazel's leaving us the key for her Airbnb, but I won't be able to take you over there until after I close up at five. Think you can hang on until then?"

"Oh, sure," she replied at once. "I'll just wander around and take a look at things. I passed a cute coffee shop on the way in, and maybe I'll grab something to drink there."

That would have been a good idea, except....

"I'm afraid that Cloud Coffee closed at three," I told her. "But you should be able to get an iced tea or something at Olamendi's. It's the Mexican restaurant at the end of the block."

To my relief, Chloe didn't look too dismayed at being deprived of a latte, or whatever she'd been hoping to order at the coffee shop. "That works," she said. "I'll come back a little after five."

"See you then."

She nodded, then hoisted her fringed black purse a little higher on her shoulder as she headed out the door. As she left, Olivia came in, looking cheerful as usual.

Perfect timing.

Obviously, I wasn't going to say anything to my assistant about the unexpected arrival of my half-sister; word would probably get around town soon enough, but I didn't see any reason to speed up the spread of that information. Olivia was a great girl and had really helped me out over the past couple of months, and yet I could tell she was already half-checked out of Globe, ready to get away and start college and see more of the wider world.

Somehow, I got the feeling she was one of those who wouldn't see any need to return to her hometown and would instead set her sights on a future that provided many more opportunities.

But she was here now, and I had to be happy about that.

"Hi, Olivia," I said, glad I sounded completely normal and not as though I'd just had my long-lost half-sister walk through the shop door, "that new shipment from Llewellyn Press came in this morning. Do you think you could unpack it for me?"

Chloe came back a few minutes after five. I'd told Olivia she could leave right on the hour since there wasn't any real tidying up that needed to be done, and she headed out, obviously happy that she'd still get paid for time she could now use for homework, or maybe just hanging out. After all, she'd already been accepted to her school of choice and was probably trying to skate by this last semester without having to exert herself too much.

And although I knew that having Chloe stay at the house wasn't an option, not with the baby so close to greeting the world, I also knew I needed to do my best to still be a gracious hostess, despite the way she'd appeared out of nowhere. That meant bringing her to the house for dinner, even though I certainly hadn't planned to have any guests. Luckily, I had a big batch of chili going in the crockpot, which would be plenty to feed all of us.

Unless she was vegan, in which case I'd just have to throw together a salad for her or something.

Anyway, I'd texted Calvin that my half-sister had shown up in Globe and that I'd be bringing her home for dinner, and although his return text had been startled, he would never have told me that wasn't a very good idea. The Standingbears were very big on family, even when they showed up on your doorstep with no warning.

"How was downtown?" I asked her as she approached the counter. I'd told Olivia I would lock up, knowing that I needed to keep the front door open for a few minutes past five. In fact, I got out the key even as Chloe was replying to my question.

"Good," she said. "I got some iced tea at Olamendi's like you suggested, and then I kind of wandered. That Sundowner Gallery place has some nice stuff. I especially liked the paintings by an artist named Hazel Marr."

I allowed myself a smile. "Hazel is an amazing

artist," I agreed as I carefully lowered myself from the stool where I'd been sitting. "She's my friend who owns the Airbnb."

"Wow, she is?" Chloe responded, looking impressed. "Does she have any of her art at the house?"

"No," I said, and my half-sister's expression fell a bit. "She decided to take out the original paintings because she didn't know whether it was a good idea to keep such valuable pieces hanging there when she didn't know how people would treat them."

Chloe pursed her lips. "I suppose I can understand that. But it's still cool that I'll be able to stay at her place."

"I think you'll like it." By then, I was able to make my way to the front door so I could lock up —good thing, because I'd spied a couple who looked like they were probably in their middle forties beginning to make their leisurely way down the sidewalk toward the store. Under other circumstances, I might have been fine with waiting and closing up shop until they'd had a chance to browse, but today I only wanted to make sure Chloe and I were able to get out of there on time.

Once the door was settled, I went back to the cash register and stowed the key in its spot under the cash drawer. I had a duplicate on the key ring I carried with me at all times, but I kept this one here in case of emergency, since I could always count on my friend Victoria to open the shop if necessary, thanks to the way the same key unlocked the door that opened on the rear lobby and the one to her studio upstairs as well.

"You'll need to follow me," I said. "Are you parked out back?"

"Yep," Chloe replied cheerfully. "I wasn't sure about the street parking, so I thought it would be safer to use the parking lot. There were lots of spaces."

Something that might have been a marvel to a person from overcrowded Southern California but was par for the course around here. A lot of people liked to park out on Bridge Street, so there were many days when it was only my white Jeep Renegade and Victoria's bright red Mercedes SUV holding court out back.

Today, though, a metallic gray Volkswagen Beetle was parked a couple of spaces away from my Jeep, and an odd little pang went through me. I'd driven a similar car for years, although mine had been the Denim edition convertible, and this one wasn't quite so fancy, although meticulously maintained. A while back, I'd given up my Beetle because it just wasn't suited to driving on the rough road out to the house every day, but even though I loved the Jeep and had been glad of its four-wheel drive on more than one occasion, I still found myself missing my VW from time to time.

"Your car?" I asked with a nod toward the little gray Beetle, and Chloe nodded.

"Yeah, I had to put in a lot of hours at Chipotle to pay for it."

She still wore a small smile, so I guessed she didn't have too much of a problem with having to earn her way toward vehicle ownership. It made sense, I supposed; a high school music teacher probably didn't earn enough to be buying cars for his kids, even if he'd held the same position for a long time and was at the top of his pay scale. I could relate, since I'd had to work hard to afford my own car in high school, a beat-up Sentra with nearly a quarter-million miles on the odometer by the time I traded it in for my brand-new Beetle.

"They're great cars," I said. "I had one of my own up until a year or so ago. But it just wasn't up to dealing with country roads on a regular basis."

"You live out in the country?" Chloe asked.

"Sort of," I replied. "Our house is on the east side of town, a couple of miles off the highway." Although the day had been sunny enough, I could feel the wind starting to pick up, and the air was cooling noticeably as the sun slipped toward the horizon. "But let's get you over to the Airbnb."

She seemed amenable to that suggestion and headed toward her VW while I laboriously clambered behind the wheel of the Jeep. Each day, that particular task got more and more difficult, but I stubbornly continued to drive myself to work even though I'd had offers from several people to play chauffeur.

No, I wanted to hold on to that small piece of freedom while I still could.

I drove slowly so Chloe wouldn't have any trouble keeping up. Since it was a drive of only a half mile or so, it didn't take too long for us to reach Hazel's Airbnb, a cute little cottage of only a bit more than a thousand square feet. She'd clearly been preparing for spring, because I noted several new annuals blooming in the flowerbeds out front, even as the daffodils and irises had already begun to make their yearly appearance.

There was a garage, but Hazel kept that for storing supplies and spare furniture. I parked out front and hoped Chloe would get the hint that it was okay to pull into the driveway, even if the garage was off-limits. She seemed to understand, because rather than parking behind me, she turned into the drive and then shut off the engine.

"It's adorable!" she exclaimed as I clambered out of my Renegade's driver's seat and closed the door behind me. "I don't think I've ever seen houses like this in the Valley."

Probably not, since the vast majority of my old stomping grounds had been built after World War

2, and the houses tended to be stucco, not little bungalows with yellow-painted siding and cheerful green shutters.

"No," I said. "There are places like this in the older parts of L.A., but I remember the Valley being pretty much ranchers and McMansions as far as the eye can see."

Chloe chuckled. "It is pretty vanilla. This place seems to have a lot more character."

Well, that it did. While some parts of Globe still looked kind of rough, the street where Hazel's Airbnb was located was lined with '20s-vintage houses that had also been restored, so the overall effect was pretty much postcard-perfect.

"Let's go inside," I said. "I think you'll like the decor, too."

Because even though Hazel had taken down her original artwork, all the furnishings in their cheery shades of green and blue and yellow remained, and she'd made sure that the canvas prints she'd hung to replace her art still worked beautifully in the space.

"I think it's the cutest place I've ever seen," Chloe declared. She'd been carrying an oversized weekender bag in addition to her fringed purse, and she set it down now on the flowered rug as she glanced around the living room. "It's obvious she chose everything in here carefully. Why doesn't she live here instead of renting it out?"

"She got married a while back to a man who owns a ranch outside town," I explained. "So she decided to keep the cottage as an income property rather than sell it."

I stopped there, though—there wasn't any point in telling my half-sister that long ago, this house had also belonged to my friend Archie, way back in the 1950s before a vengeful witch turned him into a cat for daring to spurn her advances. The curse had been broken thanks to Archie falling in love with Victoria Parrish, but while I guessed that Chloe would meet Archie and Victoria eventually, there was no way in the world I'd divulge those secrets without getting my friends' express permission.

"That makes sense," Chloe said, and I was relieved she didn't seem inclined to ask any further questions on the subject.

"Well, then," I went on, "now that we've got a place for you to stay, Calvin and I were hoping you'd come to the house for dinner tonight. I've got a big batch of chili going, and I'll make cornbread muffins."

Not for the first time, my half-sister's gaze went to my rounded belly. It seemed clear to me that she didn't think I should be doing much of anything except ordering takeout at this point.

However, she seemed to realize that commenting on my advanced pregnancy wouldn't be very diplomatic, because she only said, "All that sounds great. My schedule's been kind of weird lately, so I've been eating a lot of takeout. A home-cooked meal would be fab...as long as it's not too much trouble."

"It isn't," I assured her. "And since our gravel road can be kind of rough for regular cars, I can drive you and then have Calvin bring you back here."

"Are you sure?" Chloe returned, looking dubious. "I don't want to be an inconvenience, especially with showing up out of the blue like this."

"You're not an inconvenience," I assured her. Then, keeping my tone gentle, I added, "Is there anything you want to tell me about why you're here?"

Because for all I knew, she'd argued with her parents and had decided it seemed better to get out of town and be around someone who still technically counted as family, even if I'd never been a part of her life before now.

Her chin went up, and I could practically see her jaw harden with resolve.

"Yes," she said. "There is something else. I know I have gifts, but I don't really know what to do with them."

A pause, and then she spoke again.

"I want you to teach me how to be a witch."

Chapter 3

ONE STEP AT A TIME

"YOU WANT ME TO *WHAT?*" I BLURTED, startled enough by my half-sister's declaration that I wasn't overly concerned about how tactful my response might have sounded.

However, she didn't seem upset by my shocked tone, and repeated patiently, "I want you to teach me how to be a witch. You worked for years as a psychic in L.A., and it's obvious you're still being all witchy here with that shop of yours. I feel like there's so much more I could do if I only had someone to show me the ropes."

Because her expression was so hopeful, I knew I could never respond with a flat denial, even as one part of my brain thought it took a lot of guts to make such a request of a woman who clearly was about to give birth any day now and might have had a few more important things to occupy her time.

So I pulled in a breath and said, "Chloe, I'm not sure if that's the sort of thing you can really teach someone. It's not as if I had anyone to help me. I just sort of found my own path."

She crossed her arms and her lips compressed slightly. But to my relief, she sounded calm enough as she replied, "I've read lots about witchcraft, and it sounds as if people either learn from their family members or find a coven to work with. It's not as though they know all this stuff out of the blue."

"Some people seek out help and guidance from others," I agreed. "Everyone's route to the source is different, though. For me, I didn't have anyone like that. I just read books and did my best to find my way. Maybe your talents need something else. All I'm saying is that I'm not sure I'm the right person to teach you...especially with everything I have going on in my life."

Her head drooped a little. "I get it," she said. "Honestly, if I'd known you were about to have a baby, I would never have come here and bugged you. But now...." The words trailed off, and she uncrossed her arms and instead planted her hands on her hips. "Now, I don't know what I should do. I really don't want to be in Northridge."

Well, I could understand that. There came a time in almost everyone's life when they had to decide whether to continue with the status quo or whether it was time to forge a new path, whatever that might turn out to be. I'd had that decision thrust on me after learning Lucien Dumond was hot on my trail, and it seemed the same sort of turning point had presented itself to Chloe, even if she wasn't quite ready to tell me what that turning point was.

"I'm not saying you need to go back to California," I replied. "You can stay here for as long as you need to."

She glanced around the living room with its whimsical floral sofa and lighthearted color scheme, and again something about her seemed to droop. "It's really cute," she said. "But I don't think I could afford this place for more than a couple of days."

Did she really think I was going to ask her to pay for the Airbnb when it had been my idea for her to stay here?

Apparently so, or she wouldn't be looking so disconsolate.

"The house is my treat," I said, and her dark gray eyes flared with surprise. "I certainly don't expect you to pay for it, not when it was my idea in the first place. And while Hazel has a booking later in the month, you still have several weeks when you can stay here as you try to get things figured out."

"But I want to do something to help," Chloe

protested. "I didn't come here just so I could freeload off you. Yes, I wanted your advice on all this witchy stuff, but once I saw you had a store, I thought maybe I could work for you...if you needed an extra pair of hands."

An extra pair of hands? Definitely—and much more than that, if she was up to the task. She'd said she'd worked at Chipotle, so she obviously had experience working with the public, but that wasn't quite the same thing as having to manage a New Age store all by herself.

I knew I was getting way ahead of myself, especially considering how reticent I'd been to hire anyone else after the whole Melanie Knowles debacle. Still, sometimes we needed to stop and pay attention to the messages the universe was beaming to us, and in this case, it sure felt as though some higher power had decided to take pity on me and send the one person who might keep me from having to close Once in a Blue Moon after all.

"Maybe," I allowed, and then smiled. "Why don't you tell me about your experience?"

As it turned out, Chloe had been an assistant manager at Chipotle during her last year of college, so she knew more about dealing with inventory and placing orders for stock than I'd originally thought. It wouldn't be too hard for her to learn the nuances of managing the shop, and I had to imagine the pace would be much, much slower.

First things first, though. After she explained some of what her work had been like, I realized it was time for us to head out of town if I was going to have even a prayer of getting those cornbread muffins together in time. Chloe climbed into the passenger seat of my Renegade and glanced around somewhat wistfully.

"My friend Andrea bought one of these last year," she said. "She really likes it. But the only way she could afford the car was to have her parents give her the down payment, and there was no way I'd ask mine to give me that kind of money."

"They're strict about that sort of stuff?" I asked, curious despite myself. It was one thing for me to be all noble and pretend I didn't care what Jordan Fairfield had done with his life, but I knew deep down that I had a burning curiosity to know what the man was really like, how he interacted with his family.

"Strict?" Chloe repeated, then shook her head. "I don't know if 'strict' is the right word. They're just careful with money. My brother Justin and I always had jobs once we were old enough to work. Actually, after he graduated from college a couple of years ago, he went to work full-time for the computer company he'd been with since he was a senior in high school. I guess it makes sense—teachers don't exactly earn the same as doctors and lawyers, even though they probably should."

While I agreed with her on that point, I couldn't help saying, "Your mother doesn't work?"

"She does now," Chloe responded. "But when Justin and I were little, she stayed home. It wasn't until after I was in first grade that she got certified as an EKG tech, and that's what she does for a living."

Somehow I guessed that EKG technicians didn't make piles of money, either, although I knew it wasn't my place to ask. The picture I was getting from Chloe was that of a solidly middle-class family, one that had been able to afford a home in a decent area and have a modest lifestyle, but definitely not with the kind of extra money lying around that would have enabled them to go on lavish vacations or buy fancy cars for their children.

I couldn't help contrasting this scenario with what I'd learned about Tom's kids' upbringing—private schools, brand-new cars when they turned sixteen, their every need pretty much catered to. The result had been a couple of people I couldn't help thinking of as anything except spoiled brats, even though they were now in their thirties...and even though I, as someone who liked to believe she'd done some serious work on herself, shouldn't have been thinking of them in such judgmental terms.

But man, did they rub me the wrong way.

"Well, I really loved my Bug," I said. "But in a minute, you'll see why I needed to switch over to four-wheel drive."

In fact, the turn-off for the narrow lane that led to the house was coming up right then, so I slowed down and made the turn. The second we were off the highway, we began jouncing our way along, the Jeep's automatic four-wheel drive handling the washboard road with aplomb, even if it wasn't the smoothest ride in the world.

"I see what you mean," Chloe remarked with a grin. She reached up to grab the "Jesus handle" overhead, although her smile remained in place.

"We'll probably get the drive resurfaced before the monsoon rains come this summer," I said, slowing down a bit so my stomach wouldn't continue to smack into the steering wheel. "But we've had some cold nights, so we wanted to make sure we were past any freezes before we started the work."

"You have to pay for the maintenance? I didn't see any signs saying it was a private road."

Clearly, my half-sister paid attention to what was going on around her. "Technically, it isn't," I replied. "But ours is the only house on this lane, and it's actually on tribal lands. It's just easier to take care of it ourselves instead of having to submit a request to the elders."

I didn't bother to point out that even such a big project wouldn't be too much of a hit to our budget, mostly because I didn't see the need to go in depth about my finances to someone I'd just met, long-lost sister or no. Most people in town knew I'd inherited some kind of money, but the exact amount was something I never talked about.

Chloe gave a thoughtful nod, and we continued the rest of the way in silence...which wasn't for very long, since the house was only a hundred yards or so down the drive. I pushed the remote for the garage door and we pulled inside, then got out so we could walk over to the house.

I could tell she was keenly interested in everything, from the overall architecture of the pueblo-style adobe house to the band of cottonwoods that followed the line of the creek at the edge of the property. It was too early in the year for them to have leafed out, but the branches had a thin film of green indicating that they intended to come to life soon.

As soon as I opened the front door, my little long-haired chihuahua, Sadie, came bounding into the entryway, her flag of a tail swishing this way and that. And she went right up to Chloe, who bent down so she could scratch behind my pup's wispy ears.

"What an adorable dog! What's her name?"

"Sadie," I replied, inwardly relieved that the dog seemed to have taken to Chloe right away. Like most dogs, Sadie was a pretty good judge of character, and if she liked my half-sister, then it seemed likely the girl wasn't hiding any deep, dark secrets.

"Hi, Sadie," Chloe said, and gave the dog a final caress of her ears before she straightened again. "I'm very happy to meet you."

Sadie's tail kept going, and she followed the two of us into the living room, where Chloe set her purse down on the hearth.

"I think you've made a new friend," I said, and my half-sister's mouth turned up in a lopsided smile.

"We always had dogs around," she replied. "Our cocker mix, Buster, just passed a few months ago, and my parents are trying to decide when they should adopt a new dog."

"I'm so sorry," I said. "That's such a hard thing to go through."

Chloe only inclined her head, acknowledging my comment but clearly not wanting to reply. I'd never had pets growing up because my mother and I had lived in a series of apartments with strict no-animals policies, so I'd never dealt with such a loss personally. Over the years, though, I'd seen enough friends go through the grieving process over a beloved pet that I knew how difficult it could be.

Thank the Goddess that Sadie was a young dog, only a little over two years old, so we had plenty of years left to enjoy her company.

But then Chloe seemed to shake it off, saying, "Is there anything I can do to help you in the kitchen?"

"Not really," I replied, knowing she'd changed the topic on purpose. "Although it would be great if you could set the table. I'll show you where everything is."

Looking much more cheerful, she followed me into the kitchen, where I pointed out the drawers that contained the placemats and table settings before I headed over to the walk-in pantry to gather all the ingredients for the muffins. While I fetched a bowl from the cupboard, she went ahead and got the table ready, obviously happy to be of some use.

That was why, when Calvin came home some ten minutes later, the table was set and I was just popping the muffins in the oven. Chloe and I had been chatting about the store and how I'd found it via an online real estate listing, but I broke off at once so I could make the necessary introductions.

"Calvin, this is my sister, Chloe Fairfield," I said, and he reached out to shake her hand.

"It's very nice to meet you," he said in his warm, deep voice.

"Nice to meet you, too," she returned, looking awed. I supposed I shouldn't have been too surprised by that; although various comments I'd made had let her know my husband was chief of the tribal police, she probably hadn't been expecting someone six and a half feet tall with black hair to his waist and the kind of looks that should have put him in front of a camera.

But they hadn't, and striking as he was, my husband was very happy to simply be the chief of police for his tribe and to live a quiet existence...or at least, as quiet as it could be with a wife who couldn't seem to prevent herself from stumbling into murder investigations.

However, everything had been quiet since the holidays, when I'd helped Josie with figuring out who had murdered one of the contestants in her High Country Holiday Brewing Competition, and I thought maybe the universe had decided to take it easy on me for a while, considering I had a very important event of my own coming up soon.

And because Calvin and I had long ago agreed that we should never keep secrets from one another, I thought I might as well say, "Chloe found me using her Tarot. It sounds like we have quite a bit in common."

"Oh?" my husband responded, looking amused. "Are you another hedgewitch like Selena?"

Both of Chloe's eyebrows lifted, but she said in similarly light tones, "Probably not. I like reading Tarot and that kind of thing, but the witchiest thing about me is the way I sometimes see stuff in my dreams."

This was the first time I'd heard anything about that, but I told myself it wasn't too strange. After all, my younger sister and I had only met a few hours earlier, and even then, the majority of the time since then had been occupied with keeping watch on the store. It wasn't as if we'd had the opportunity to sit down and spill our entire life stories.

"The future?" I asked, knowing I sounded a bit startled.

Her shoulders lifted. "Sometimes. Or sometimes I see things that are happening as I dream about them. Like, in my junior year of high school, I had a dream that a group of my friends got into a car accident coming back from the homecoming game. I was supposed to be there with them, but I got strep throat and had to stay home. The next day, I found out my dream was real...right down to the color of the truck that T-boned their SUV."

"I hope they were okay," Calvin said.

That was my husband to a T. He wasn't fazed by talk about locating people with the Tarot or having true dreams, but he needed to know that the group involved in the car accident had survived the crash just fine.

"They were," Chloe said. "I mean, Trey and Lola had broken arms because they were on the side where the truck hit them, but the police caught the guy—he'd been driving drunk—and he's in jail now. And my friends mostly just had fun having people sign their casts."

Well, I supposed that was one way of making lemonade from what must have been a terrifying incident. And while it was the kind of story some would-be psychics might have concocted to make themselves sound more impressive, I didn't think that was what was happening here. For one thing, Chloe had spoken simply about the situation, without any embellishment, and for another, just as she finished her comment, her aura flickered into existence above her head for a second or two before disappearing again. It was a gorgeous shade of dark pine green, washed with deep teal around the edges, and definitely not the aura of someone telling a lie.

No, it was the aura of someone who could be trusted.

Something inside me relaxed then. Yes, I already had Sadie's reaction to Chloe to let me know my little sister was on the up and up, but seeing with my own eyes that she was no more than who she seemed to be made me feel much better about the way she'd appeared in Globe out of nowhere.

Calvin smiled, and the next few minutes were all about grating cheese and getting a pitcher of lemon water from the fridge—and me apologizing that I'd been avoiding alcohol and caffeine, for obvious reasons, and that I hoped Chloe wouldn't mind too much.

"It's fine," she said. "It was a long drive here, so I don't think I would have wanted anything else to drink even if you had it. A glass of wine would've probably made me face-plant in my chili."

That remark made Calvin and me both grin. He got the muffins out of the oven for me so I wouldn't have to bend down again, and as soon as they were tipped into a basket and the big crock of chili had been carried into the dining room and set down on some hot pads, we were ready to eat.

A moment of quiet as we dished up the food—with Sadie scurrying from place to place, wondering which of us would be the softest touch for scrounging some morsels during the meal—and then everyone took their first bites.

"This is the best chili I've ever had," Chloe declared once she'd washed down her food with a swallow of water. "What's your secret?"

"A kitchen witch never divulges her secrets," Calvin remarked with a grin, and Chloe raised an eyebrow.

"Selena, I thought you said you were a hedgewitch."

"Well, it's all kind of loosely defined," I said. "I love to cook and do things in the kitchen, but I'm also a solitary witch and self-taught, which is part of what defines a hedgewitch, so I suppose I've just sort of mashed everything together."

Now it was Calvin's turn for an eyebrow lift. "'Solitary'?" he echoed. "After living with me for the past year and a half?"

About all I could do was grin. "Not that kind of solitary," I told him. "It just means that I don't practice with a coven."

"Makes sense," he said, and broke a muffin in half so he could spread some butter on it.

The baby kicked then and I started, then put a hand on my belly. So far he—or she—had been pretty quiescent today, but maybe the scent of chili and cornbread had been a kind of wake-up call.

"Evening gymnastics routine?" Calvin asked, and I nodded.

"Something like that. But I'd rather have it happen at dinner than 3 a.m."

After hearing this exchange, Chloe said, "When are you due?"

"On the sixteenth," I replied, and she relaxed almost imperceptibly. True, that was still not all that far off in the future, but I could tell she was glad I hadn't said the baby was supposed to be here the day after tomorrow. "Speaking of which," I went on, looking back over at Calvin, "Chloe and I were talking earlier, and she told me she'd like to help out at the store while I'm on leave."

My husband, who'd been looking fairly relaxed up until then, at once sat up a little straighter in his chair. While he didn't frown—he was far too polite to make such a show of disapproval in front of our guest—I could tell he wasn't as thrilled as I'd hoped he would be at my revelation.

However, his tone was even enough as he said, "That's really nice of you, Chloe. So, you're planning on staying in town for a while?"

"That was my thought," she said. A flicker that came and went in her eyes told me she'd picked up on his body language and wasn't quite sure what to make of it. However, she still sounded upbeat and cheerful as she went on, "I always had this feeling that SoCal wasn't going to be it for me, you know? And then when I found Selena in Globe, it felt as if the universe was guiding me here somehow. That probably sounds kind of crazy."

A corner of his mouth lifted, and I knew he was thinking about the way I'd arrived in our small town, guided here by the cards as well. "Not as crazy as you might think," he replied. "And I can see why getting out of L.A. might seem like a good idea. I've only been there once, but that was enough for me."

"Calvin's not a city boy," I said, knowing my own mouth wore a similar smile. "And that's fine—coming here to Globe was the right thing for me.

L.A. is an amazing place, but it can really wear you out."

Chloe broke off a piece of her cornbread muffin and spread a modest amount of butter on it. "That's exactly it. I was just...tired. I knew I needed something different in my life."

That comment might have caused just the slightest flicker of my husband's eyes toward me, accompanied by a quirk of his lips that I doubted anyone else would have been able to detect. It was probably a bit difficult for him to believe that someone as young as Chloe Fairfield would already have been overcome by *ennui* at the prospect of spending the rest of her life in the big city, but at the same time, I'd grown up in the Valley as well and knew what it felt like to be overwhelmed by the crush of population in the greater Los Angeles area.

And that didn't even take into account how the cost of living just kept going up and up. When I moved out when I was a little past nineteen, at least I'd been able to earn enough to pay for a modest studio apartment. These days, unless you were making six figures right out of school, you'd never be able to afford a place of your own in L.A.

No wonder Chloe had still been living at home...and no wonder she was looking forward to spending the next few weeks in Hazel's darling vacation rental.

It wasn't a permanent solution, but for now, I was just glad the place had been available at all. For a while, I'd thought that Sofia Barnes, one of the competitors in Josie's brewing contest back in December, would settle into Hazel's place, but it turned out that the old hardware store Sofia had bought for her brewpub start-up had an apartment space above it, and it just made sense for her to fix it up at the same time and be right where the action was, so to speak.

"And I made it to assistant manager at Chipotle while I was working my way through school," Chloe went on. "So, while it's not exactly the same as running a New Age shop, I've got lots of customer-facing experience and know how to handle the books at a store."

Calvin gave a grave nod, although I could tell he was still inwardly amused. "This isn't a job interview, Chloe," he said. "If Selena believes you're the right person to watch over the store while she's out on leave, then I know it's going to be fine. Her instincts are impeccable."

I sent him a grateful smile, and my sister seemed to relax slightly, even as she looked a little wistful. Was she surprised that Calvin would be so openly supportive of my decision? Hard to say; I certainly didn't know her very well yet, and I knew even less about her family dynamics, whether her parents were equal partners or whether my bio-dad took his role as man of the house seriously.

Which seemed as though it would be a complete about-face, considering he'd been a head-banging drummer in a metal band when he hooked up with my mother, but people often changed in strange and mysterious ways.

"So I think it's settled," I said, and sent an encouraging smile my little sister's way. "Tomorrow, you can come with me to the store and get started."

Chapter 4

SIBLING SORORITY

ANY MISGIVINGS I MIGHT HAVE HAD ABOUT installing Chloe as my replacement at the store were quickly erased the next morning. She was quick and eager to learn, and already knew a great deal about the various Tarot and oracle decks, telling me she was far more than a mere dabbler.

"Oh, I own about fifteen decks," she said after she'd helped a pair of tourists from Phoenix choose a Moonology deck and some moonstone and amethyst pocket crystals to go with it. "I started using them in middle school."

"And your parents didn't mind?" I inquired. No reason why they should, but people could harbor odd prejudices.

At once, Chloe shook her head. "They're pretty easygoing. Their only real rules were to get good grades, stay off drugs, and not get pregnant."

I couldn't help smiling, since my mother had guided my teenage years with just about the same set of rules. But then, I supposed they were pretty universal.

"Did you go to the Tarot because of your dreams?" I asked next.

Her expression brightened, letting me know she was glad I'd figured it out so quickly.

"Yep, that's exactly what happened," she replied. "I started having them when I was around eleven, so I tried to do some research online about psychics and that kind of stuff. I found people on YouTube doing Tarot readings, and I got hooked. It wasn't until high school that I started working with oracle cards, too, but Tarot's always been my main thing."

We had to break off the conversation there, because Josie entered the shop right then, today wearing a turquoise blue blazer and matching skirt that went much better with her fiery hair than the hot pink she'd had on the day before.

Immediately, her gaze moved to Chloe, frankly questioning, and I knew the moment had arrived.

Thanks to the way Josie was able to spread news all over town in what felt like the blink of an eye, I knew most of Globe would know within the hour that my long-lost half-sister had shown up out of the blue just in time to keep me from shutting down the store for an indefinite period.

"Hi, Josie," I said. "This is Chloe Fairfield. She's my little sister from L.A."

I deliberately introduced her that way because even though we didn't share the same mother, we still had Jordan Fairfield's blood running through our veins. There didn't seem to be much point in continuing to make the distinction that we were only half-sisters.

For just a second, Josie's light blue eyes flared with surprise, but then she smiled and came forward with her usual bustling energy.

"So nice to meet you, Chloe," she said. "I'm Josie Woodrow."

"She's the mayor," I put in. "But before that, she was the person who sold me this store."

"And I'm still in real estate," Josie added. "So you just let me know if you're in the market for a house around here."

That sort of offer was pretty much par for the course for Josie, but Chloe's startled expression told me she definitely hadn't expected the conversation to take that kind of left turn quite so quickly.

"She's staying at Hazel's Airbnb for now," I said, keeping my tone light...and also hoping Josie would get the hint that it wasn't really the time to be talking about buying real estate when my sister had only shown up in town the day before. "But we'll let you know. The important thing is that Chloe came here just in time to help me out with the store. She'll be running things while I'm out on leave."

If Josie was at all surprised by the arrangement, she didn't show it. No, she only nodded and asked, "Does that mean the fifty percent off sale is canceled?"

Trust her to worry about something like that. Lips quirking with amusement, I said, "No, I'll keep it going through the end of the week, just as I advertised. It'll help to clear out some old stock that's been sitting around for longer than I would have liked. And then Chloe can order new inventory...kind of like a spring cleaning for Once in a Blue Moon."

"That sounds like an excellent idea," Josie said. "And it's wonderful that you came at just the right time, Chloe. But I have a meeting I need to get to —very nice to meet you."

And with that she headed out, leaving a drift of Chanel No. 5 in her wake.

Chloe blinked. "She's kind of a force of nature, huh?"

I couldn't help grinning. "You have no idea."

As I'd expected, word spread fast, saving me the effort of having to reach out to everyone and let them know what was going on at the shop. Hazel dropped in to meet my sister, gave me an approving nod, and then headed out again. Victoria also came down from her studio so she could make her introductions with the person who would soon be running the store, and even Archie deigned to come by a little after one o'clock, since he didn't have another dance class to teach until three.

His was the opinion I worried about the most. Although he would never come right out and admit it, I knew he looked on me as the sister he'd never had, just as I considered him a sort of found brother, and he was fiercely protective of me. After what had happened with Melanie Knowles, there was every chance he'd tell me I was out of my mind for inviting Chloe into my life so quickly when I knew so little about her.

Well, I wasn't being quite as careless as it might have looked on the surface. That morning when Calvin went to work, he did a quick background check on Chloe, just to make sure I wasn't the victim of a particularly clever con artist. He messaged me soon after, telling me that everything seemed to be on the up and up—she'd been born in Northridge Medical Center, had attended school in the local district, and graduated from Cal State Northridge...the same university I'd dropped out of more than ten years earlier after realizing a college diploma wasn't what I needed in life...and that her parents had owned the same house since

1998 and were employed in exactly the professions she'd described.

While I really hadn't had any reason to doubt her—the aura I'd seen hovering over her head the day before had told me everything I needed to know—it was still reassuring to have some solid proof that she truly was Jordan Fairfield's daughter and not someone trying to worm their way into my life so they could get their hands on my money.

Again, I made the necessary introductions, and although Archie seemed surprised by Chloe's sudden appearance, he only said it was nice to meet her. At the same time, I could tell my sister was impressed by Archie, who wasn't exactly the sort of person you'd expect to find in tiny Globe, not with his impeccable clothing and the sort of handsome blond looks that seemed as though they would have been put to better use in some kind of classic film.

"So, what brings you to Globe?" Archie asked, and even though I could tell he was being on his best behavior, it was also somewhat obvious to me that he wasn't going to head back to his dance studio until he had some answers that satisfied him.

"Finding Selena," Chloe said frankly. "I mean, I knew she existed, but my father never talked much about her. I graduated from college a semester early, and it just seemed like the right time to look her up."

Archie's expression didn't change, but he

nodded, as if pleased to hear that my unexpected little sister was no slouch in the academics department. Back in the day, before he was turned into a cat, he'd been a history teacher, and although he'd left that profession behind, I knew he still had very little use for ignorance.

Instead, his gaze shifted back toward me. "And you, Selena—why didn't you ever go in search of your little sister?"

A valid enough question, but one I wished he'd asked in private. I honestly didn't know how much Chloe's father had said about the way he'd made it clear he wanted to live his own life, one that didn't involve my mother...or the child he'd fathered after a single drunken night of passion.

"Oh, my bio-father didn't want to have much to do with us," I said lightly. "He paid child support, and that was it. Which is fine. It's never a good idea to force people to have a life together just because of a single mistake they made."

A golden-brown eyebrow lifted. "You see yourself as a mistake?"

"Of course not," I returned at once, even as Chloe began to frown, as though annoyed on my behalf. "I just mean the hook-up that started the whole thing. It was my mother's choice to keep me, and Jordan did the right thing by sending money. There wasn't any need to make him do more than that."

Although Archie had been living in the twenty-first century as a man for more than a year, he still had a hard time with our much more casual attitudes toward sex. In this particular case, though, it seemed he'd realized it wouldn't be a very good idea to push me further on the topic.

"I understand," he said, and even managed to smile. "Then I suppose it's a very good thing that the two of you were able to meet as adults—and that Chloe is in a position to help with the shop."

"I'm looking forward to it," she said. "And I'm super glad that I got here at just the right time. The universe definitely guided me where I needed to be."

Since that was exactly the sort of woo-woo statement I would have made in a similar situation, Archie's expression turned sour. However, his tone was pleasant enough as he said, "Yes, it does seem as though you were a godsend. And if you ever need anything while Selena is out on leave, I'm just next door—and my wife Victoria is upstairs."

"Oh, Victoria's your wife?" Chloe asked, looking a little confused. True, they had different last names, and Victoria hadn't mentioned anything about Archie, probably because she'd come down to say hi to Chloe in between client meetings and hadn't had any real time to go into details.

"Yes," he said, obviously proud to be able to

claim such an accomplished woman as his partner in life. "She sometimes helps out with the studio when she has the time." He paused there and gave Chloe a searching look. "I don't suppose you dance."

"What, like ballet?" she said, even more befuddled.

"Ballroom," he explained patiently. "Waltz... tango...foxtrot. That sort of thing."

Chloe let out a chuckle, then paused, as if she realized laughing in response to his comment might not have been the most polite thing to do. "Oh, no," she said. "I've got two left feet."

"That can be fixed," he said, something in his tone telling me that my little sister was going to end up in one of his beginning ballroom classes whether she liked it or not. But then he glanced over at me and added, "At any rate, I'll let you two get back to it. I'm sure you have a good deal to show Chloe before the big day arrives."

"Oh, lots," I said. "But we've still got some time."

"Hopefully," he said, his tone now ominous. His gaze moved to Chloe and he added, "It was very nice to meet you. Remember, I'm just next door if you need anything."

And then he went out, moving past a couple of people who looked as though they'd taken a break during a hiking trip to come downtown and do some browsing, judging by their cargo shorts and sturdy boots.

Since they headed immediately for the book section, Chloe seemed to think it was safe to continue our conversation. "Are all your friends so...dramatic?"

I couldn't help chuckling. "Well, Archie and Josie are definitely their own people. But you also met Hazel and Victoria. They're pretty normal, right?"

Chloe shook her head. "They're more low-key. But since Victoria looks like a movie star and Hazel is some kind of world-class artist, I'm not sure I'd use 'normal' to describe them."

Fair enough. Still smiling, I said, "I guess Globe just isn't a 'normal' kind of place."

The rest of the day went smoothly, though, with Joyce Lewis also stopping by to meet Chloe—and to drop off a new batch of candles. I showed my sister how to log everything into the inventory system and where to store things in the stock room, and ended up thinking that this was all going to work out just perfectly. In fact, although I'd first thought I'd stay through the end of the week just to make sure she was on top of everything, I was now beginning to wonder whether I should take only another day to get her up to speed and then go home and spend the rest of the ten days or so until I was due with my feet up on the couch, the way an eight-months-plus pregnant woman should.

Chloe was good with the customers and quick to learn how I did inventory—probably not the most efficient system in the world, but it worked—and yet it seemed that whenever I tried to ask her about her life back in Southern California, she somehow managed to give a brief answer before turning the conversation to something more innocuous, like a question about how to place an order with my two biggest vendors, Llewellyn Press and Hay House.

I supposed it was possible that she didn't want to talk about her life very much because her parents had admonished her not to divulge too much information about their family dynamics. Again, since I knew very little about Jordan Fairfield as a person, I had no idea whether he would have even laid down that sort of commandment, or whether he and his wife would have simply told Chloe to stay safe and left it at that. After all, even though she was still living at home, she was also an adult of twenty-one and paying rent to stay there. When you got right down to it, I didn't think there was much her parents could have done to prevent their daughter from doing as she liked.

One question she asked did surprise me a little, though.

"Do you ever do readings here?" she inquired after the hikers left, books on cryptozoology stowed in their bags.

"Tarot readings?" I responded, and she nodded.

"I mean, that's what you did when you lived in L.A., right?"

"I did," I said, which was only the truth. I'd made a decent living reading Tarot and sometimes using my pendulum to provide counsel to a variety of West Los Angeles types, a lot of whom worked in the film and TV industry, even if they weren't the forward-facing kind of people that anyone would have heard of. "But when I came here, I thought I'd make a fresh start, and that meant focusing on running the shop rather than being an actual psychic. I still do readings for myself and occasionally for friends if it's something they feel is important enough, but trying to read cards as part of the business would have been too much. Until I got pregnant, this was pretty much a one-person operation."

Chloe seemed to absorb all this information, her expression thoughtful. "I suppose I can see that," she said after a pause. "But maybe once you come back from leave...."

She left the sentence hanging, and yet I

thought I could guess what she was trying to say. While she was minding the store during my absence, she'd have to focus on being a shopkeeper. In the long run, though...if it turned out that she wanted to stay on...then maybe we could expand the business to having her conduct readings while I was out front working with customers, or vice versa.

"You like reading Tarot for people?" I asked, and she nodded.

"I started doing it in high school for my friends," she said. "And then in college, I worked at a couple of psychic fairs and did readings there."

An impressive resume for someone her age, since the fairs I'd attended before deciding I had a hard time focusing in crowds had been very careful about who they invited to be guest readers. Once again, I pondered whether I should ask if her parents had a problem with her attending those sorts of events—I loved my psychic community back in L.A., but even I'd known that the fairs could attract some fairly fringe people—and then I decided it wasn't any of my business. From what I'd been able to tell, Chloe had genuine talent, and it seemed clear enough to me that her parents hadn't wanted to stand in her way.

"Well, it's something we can talk about when the time comes," I said, and she seemed to get the hint that I wasn't about to start making promises, not with a baby due any day now.

Olivia came in around three-thirty and I introduced the two girls. They seemed to hit it off right away, which was a relief, especially since I'd wondered if Olivia would worry that I planned to let her go now that I had Chloe here to help out. However, I had no intention of doing such a thing, figuring that it would be easier for both of them to have someone else here for at least part of the day. Besides, I knew Olivia had been counting on the money she was saving from her part-time job to help her get situated in her new apartment, and it wouldn't have been fair to cut her off with no warning.

With everything that had been going on, I was kind of blindsided when my phone rang at four—a call from my mother, who'd been expected in town that afternoon, even though she hadn't known for sure exactly when she and Tom would arrive at their home at the east end of Globe.

As soon as I saw her number, an uneasy sensation went through my stomach that had nothing to do with the baby I was carrying. How in the world was she going to react to finding out that my sister was not only here, but had already been welcomed into my life?

It's fine, I reassured myself. *It's not as if she's been harboring some kind of undying love for*

Jordan Fairfield all these years. And she never said you couldn't look up your half-siblings, only that she didn't know whether it would be a very good idea.

Even though my inner voice sounded particularly no-nonsense, I wasn't sure whether I could believe it. After all, I'd never dealt with a situation like this before.

"Hi, Mom," I said as I touched the screen to answer the phone. Luckily, Chloe and Olivia were over by the bookcases, maybe talking about the shelving system I used. But whatever they were doing, they didn't seem to be paying any attention to me, thank the Goddess. "How are you?"

"I should be asking you that question," she said with a laugh.

"Oh, I'm fine," I told her. "Are you here in town?"

"Yes," she replied. "We got to the house about fifteen minutes ago. I thought I'd open up some windows and air out the place a little bit before I gave you a call."

My mother always had been a fresh-air fiend. If it was truly hot, then of course she'd close up everything and turn on the A/C, but she always preferred to have breezes blowing through open windows, and I couldn't really blame her for that since I was the same way.

"That's good," I said, then paused. There wasn't any way to tell her what was going on without just blurting it out, so that's what I did. "Mom, Chloe Fairfield showed up in Globe yesterday. She's a great girl, and I'm having her help me here at the store."

A pause. Then my mother said, almost blankly, "*Jordan's* Chloe?"

"Yes," I replied. "I know it's kind of a shock, but—"

"It's fine," my mother cut in. "I'm actually glad to hear that she reached out to you. How old is she now?"

"Twenty-one, I think," I said, feeling somewhat surreal. I supposed if I'd stopped to think about it, I should have known my mother would take the situation in stride. There wasn't a whole lot that fazed her...except maybe a demon infestation that had turned out to be fake in the end. Then again, at the time none of us had guessed that the terrible manifestations in the historic house she and Tom had bought were a huge lie and not actual imps from Hell. "She's staying at Hazel's Airbnb for now."

"Well, she's certainly welcome at the house if Hazel needs her rental back," my mother said. "We've got tons of space."

True enough, since the massive Victorian was more than four thousand square feet in size and had six bedrooms. All the same, I was touched that my mother had made the offer. A lot of people would have found it just a little awkward to stay under the same roof as the child of their long-ago one-night stand.

"I'll let her know," I responded, and figured I'd better leave it at that for now. "Anyway, I know we all planned to meet for dinner tonight—is it okay if I bring Chloe along? She's started to meet a few people in town, but she's definitely not at the point where she'd be getting together with friends for meals yet."

"Oh, it's fine," my mother said at once. "It'll give us a chance to all get acquainted. Tom already made reservations at the Gold Dust, but we'll just call and let them know we'll be a party of five instead of four."

"Thanks, Mom," I said, knowing I was thanking her for a whole lot more than merely changing the dinner reservations to accommodate our new guest.

"Not a problem." She paused there, then added, her tone changing subtly, "I think it's wonderful that your baby's aunt will be here when he or she comes into the world. I know Calvin has plenty of family who're awaiting the big day, but...."

"But it'll be nice to have someone else from my side of the family," I finished softly.

"Exactly. Well, we'll see you at the Gold Dust at six-thirty."

I told her it was a date, and we ended the call. As I set down the phone, my gaze moved across the room to the spot where Chloe was still standing and laughing with Olivia. We didn't have any customers in the store right then, so it wasn't as if I needed to take them to task for wasting time...not that I would have even if the situation had been different.

No, right then I was thinking about something else entirely.

I was thinking about family...and how good it was to know that mine had expanded unexpectedly but beautifully over the past two days.

Chapter 5

GOLD DUST WOMAN

CHLOE WAS MORE THAN A LITTLE surprised when I told her about our dinner plans a few minutes after my phone chat with my mother. "Your mom's really okay with me being there?" she asked, a tinge of pink touching her cheeks.

"Absolutely," I replied at once. "She made a point of including you. Remember, there aren't any hard feelings between your dad and her, so she's much more interested in getting to meet you than worrying about something that happened more than thirty years ago."

This no-nonsense description of the situation seemed to reassure Chloe, because some of the worried look left her eyes and she gave a small nod. Still, she didn't seem to be completely at ease about the prospect, since she glanced down at her black skirt and boots and said, sounding dubious, "Is the restaurant fancy? Because I didn't bring anything really special with me, just the stuff I usually wear."

"Nothing in Globe is fancy," I told her with a smile. "What you're wearing is great. I'm not planning on changing."

By that point, I was way too big to wear anything except Empire-style maternity dresses and skirts with the most forgiving elastic waistbands possible, so my wardrobe wasn't exactly what you could call extensive. The green gown I had on was one that Calvin liked a lot and was on the rotation at least once a week, but it was holding up pretty well.

"That's good," Chloe replied. "Then I won't worry about it."

Several more customers came in right then, so she hurried off to help them, leaving me to sit on my stool behind the counter. I assumed at some point they'd come up to the cash register to check out if they decided to buy anything, but for the moment, I couldn't help feeling a little superfluous.

Which was just fine by me. I'd still come in tomorrow to make sure I'd covered all the bases with Chloe, but it definitely looked as though I'd be able to hand over the reins of the business sooner than I'd expected.

Then I could truly concentrate on bringing my precious cargo safely into the world.

Even though I'd worried that the meeting at the Gold Dust casino's restaurant might still be awkward despite my mother's reassurances to the contrary, it went better than I could have expected. She'd hugged Chloe and told her she was very glad to meet her, then introduced Tom. I could tell my little sister was happy to see my mother paired off and was in what appeared to be a very successful marriage. Not that there was any chance of her ever getting back together with Jordan Fairfield, but I had a feeling Chloe had sort of viewed my mother as a loose end in her father's life nonetheless.

At dinner, they talked about life in the Valley, since my mother and Tom lived in Encino, about twenty minutes away from Chloe's childhood home in Northridge. And then when my mom could tell that Calvin and I were starting to feel a little left out of the conversation, she deftly steered the discussion back toward Globe.

"Chloe, did you know that your sister has become quite the amateur detective since moving here?"

At once, Chloe set down her steak knife and looked over me, clearly surprised. "You mean like solving murders?"

"Yes," I said. While I might have preferred to avoid that topic for a while longer, I also couldn't deny that I'd probably tracked down far more killers than most cops ever had. "I suppose the whole thing just sort of fell into my lap, but over the past couple of years it's been...how many?" I asked, turning toward Calvin, who sat next to me.

"Eleven," he supplied with a smile.

"That seems like a lot of murders for such a small town," Chloe said. "Are people around here really that bloodthirsty?"

"Well, not all those murders happened here," I told her. "One of them took place at a ballroom dance competition Archie and Victoria were attending. That was in Scottsdale."

"And most of them weren't perpetrated by actual residents of Globe," Calvin added. "They just happened to be committed here."

"Still," Chloe said, although her expression was now more thoughtful than anything. "So, do you use the Tarot to help you solve the crimes?"

"When I can," I said. "Other times, I work with my pendulum...or I consult my grandmother's spirit in my crystal ball."

I mentioned this last with a worried little glance toward my mother, since I did my best to refrain from talking about those otherworldly consultations in case it might upset her that I was communing with her dead mother's ghost. However, she didn't seem bothered by it, and in fact seemed reassured that Grandma Ellen was still out there somewhere, dispensing helpful advice.

"That is so cool," Chloe breathed. "I've only helped my friends find out if their boyfriends were cheating on them."

Somehow, I managed to prevent a smile from touching my lips. "Oh, I'm sure you've done more than that if you were working at psychic fairs."

Now it was my mother's turn to look impressed. "So, you're psychic like Selena?"

"I guess so," Chloe said with an embarrassed little lift of her shoulders. "But yes, I read cards and have visions and stuff like that."

"So, it must come from the Fairfield side of the family," Tom remarked, speaking for the first time after our initial hugs of greeting in the lobby of the restaurant. In a way, I was kind of surprised by his comment, simply because both he and my mother were very no-nonsense types, and my decidedly woo-woo outlook on life had always been a little uncomfortable for them despite the way they did their best to take it in stride.

But I supposed my track record of solving murders using less than conventional methods had proved to them that there was a whole lot more to all this psychic stuff than they could have ever imagined.

"That's what I've been thinking," Chloe said. "I guess I have a great-great-something grandmother on my father's side who was supposed to be psychic."

"Not that these things have to be hereditary," I commented as I reached for my glass of water. By that point, I'd mostly gotten used to eating a steak without a glass of red wine to accompany it, but all the same, I really couldn't wait until that blessed day six months or so from now when I could start drinking wine again. Swollen ankles and back pain were an unavoidable part of being pregnant, but I knew there was no way I was going to become a lifelong teetotaler. "I had lots of psychic friends in L.A. who didn't have anyone in their families who had any kind of extrasensory gifts. But still, I don't think it's a coincidence that both Chloe and I have some special talents in common."

My mother smiled then and reached for the glass of wine at her place setting. She and Tom had offered to share their bottle of cabernet with Chloe, an offer she'd gladly accepted. I had to remind myself that she was of drinking age, even though she looked so young...and it wasn't as if any of them had sworn off alcohol to keep me company the way Calvin had.

"Anyway," she said after taking a sip of wine, "I feel like being here with Selena will help teach me lots of things."

Calvin lifted an eyebrow, and I said, "Well, I

don't profess to be an expert, but I'll do what I can."

"I don't think Selena is going to have a lot of free time over the next few months," my mother put in. She leavened the comment with a smile, but I could tell she wanted Chloe to get the message that the baby I was carrying had to take precedence over a half-sister who'd appeared basically out of nowhere just before I was about to become a full-time mom.

Apparently realizing her misstep, Chloe said quickly, "Oh, I get it. Babies take a lot of time and energy. But I think just being around her shop and seeing how she set things up will be very educational."

Those words appeared to mollify my mother, especially since she was just as glad as the rest of us that my sister seemed willing to shoulder the entire burden of running the store so I'd be able to focus on this next, all-important stage in my life.

"I hope so," I said, keeping my tone as neutral as possible, and the conversation moved on to other subjects, including the brunch my mother would be hosting at her house that coming Saturday. I'd told everyone that I didn't want a baby shower, not when I was fully capable of buying everything I needed on my own and didn't want to put a financial burden on anyone, but my mother had insisted on having a brunch "for the girls"—

that is, Josie and Hazel and Victoria and Joyce, along with Josie's niece-in-law Terry Woodrow and Sofia Barnes. At first, Sofia had wanted to demur, since Saturdays were often the busiest days at her new brewpub, but she'd decided that she could squeeze in brunch after all, as things didn't really start to ramp up until after one or so in the afternoon.

"And of course you're invited, Chloe," my mother said. "You can just open the shop a little late on Saturday. Since everyone was expecting it to be closed altogether, I don't think anyone will mind."

Chloe's gaze moved toward me. "Is that all right, Selena?"

"Of course it is," I said, and scooped up a mouthful of baked potato. "I've closed the shop at all sorts of odd hours if I was tracking down a lead, so people are pretty much used to it by now."

My reply seemed to cheer her up, because she leaned against the back of her chair, looking relieved. "Then I'd love to come."

With that settled, we chatted some about the plans my mother had for the mansion's gardens—they were already picture-perfect, but I knew she wanted something to occupy her during the months she would be spending here in Globe—and soon enough, the end of the evening rolled around. As Calvin helped me up from my seat, the baby kicked, hard, and I couldn't help wincing.

"Everything all right?" my mother asked at once.

I could only smile. "Oh, I'm fine," I assured her. "This one's just getting restless."

"But your doctor is still saying the sixteenth is the due date," she pressed, and I nodded.

"No change in the big day," I said. "Or at least, we don't see any signs that he or she is ready to come into the world earlier than that. But babies have a mind of their own, so let's just say I don't have any plans to take off for the Bahamas in the near future."

Everyone chuckled at my remark, as I'd hoped they would, but my mother still looked a little concerned. I couldn't really blame her, not when I knew she must be thinking about my own early arrival. Her doctor had predicted I would be born at the end of June, which was part of the reason why she'd wanted to name me Selena, since I would have been a Cancer, or moon child.

But I'd had other ideas and had popped into the world right on the solstice, making me a Gemini. Despite my early appearance, she hadn't changed my name, and I was glad of that. I really couldn't imagine being anyone else.

We all walked out to our cars together, shared

hugs all around, and got into our various vehicles so we could head home. Chloe had driven herself since her Airbnb wasn't anywhere close to either Calvin's and my house or my mother and Tom's big place at the edge of town, but she drove off confidently enough.

Well, Globe wasn't so big that it took very long to get acquainted with the town, and besides, she could always have her phone guide her back to the Airbnb if necessary.

Calvin and I were both quiet on the way home, although he held my hand as he drove, clearly wanting to let me know he was there for me. This was also his last week of work, as he'd already arranged to take six weeks off from his position with the tribal police. They really couldn't spare him for any longer than that, but I told myself it would still be enough, that having him around for that first crucial month—not to mention my mother and all the rest of the Standingbear relations—would make it much easier for me to slide into motherhood.

After we went into the house and paused to give Sadie some reassuring pats and hugs after our absence, he said, "That went well."

"It did," I agreed. "Despite my mom saying it would all be okay, I still wasn't sure how she and Chloe were going to be around each other. But it all seemed pretty relaxed, which is a relief. The last thing I need is the two of them not getting along, especially with my mother planning to be here for the next couple of months."

Calvin helped me lower myself to the couch and then set a pillow just where I wanted it so I could elevate my feet. They weren't quite as swollen as they might have been, mostly because I was being careful about my salt intake and also took whatever opportunity I could to raise them to a decent height, but still, I was looking forward to the time when I wouldn't have to worry about those sorts of things.

"And Chloe being here...however long she plans to stay," he said.

Something in his voice made me tilt my head at him. "I thought you were okay with all this."

"I am," he replied, looking unruffled. He sat down in the accent chair next to the couch, which, even though it was sturdy enough, always seemed dwarfed by his oversized frame. "I told you I was fine with whatever you wanted to do, and I stand by that. Still, this is all happening kind of fast."

It was. Maybe if this baby wasn't coming in the next ten days or so, I might have taken longer to consider my decision. At the same time, every instinct I possessed was telling me Chloe was a trustworthy person and that she was the right person to take care of the store while I was on leave. True, those same instincts hadn't been functioning so well when I hired Melanie Knowles, but I was well past the brain fog of the early days of my pregnancy. Lately, I'd been feeling as sharp as ever, and I knew I could trust my gut on this one.

"I won't argue with you about that," I said. "But at the same time, I have to believe this is the right thing for all of us. I can tell Chloe needed a change of pace."

"Any chance you're going to reach out to her parents?" Calvin asked then, and I shook my head.

"Why should I? She seems young, but she's an adult. She graduated from college and is at a point where she needs to make some decisions about her future. I don't know what she said to her mother and father, but that's between them, don't you think?"

His mouth quirked. "I suppose it is. But I also think maybe your own history is coloring your judgment here. After all, you were pretty young when you left home."

"I was," I said. "And I did sit down and talk it through with my mother. It wasn't as though we didn't get along—I just knew deep down that I was ready to leave the nest, and that my mother had pretty much given up nineteen years of her life for me. It was time for her to come into her own as well."

Another instance where my instincts had guided me well, as she'd started seeing Tom a few years later, leading to their eventual marriage. I didn't think he'd been waiting for my mother to be fancy-free before he began to show an interest in her, more that the universe had arranged matters so everything would work out well for the two of them.

"I can see that," Calvin replied. "And you're right—Chloe seems like a kid, but there's no reason in the world why she shouldn't be striking out on her own at this point in her life." He paused there, then asked, his tone quite different, "Do you want to watch some TV, or would you rather head to bed?"

Only a year ago, I would have been almost offended at the suggestion that I go to bed at barely eight-thirty. These days, though, I did my best to get as much sleep as possible, sometimes as much as nine or ten hours each night.

I might as well bank as much sleep now while I could, since I knew I wasn't going to have the chance in the very near future.

"Bed," I said promptly, and he reached out so he could help me up from the sofa and down the hallway to the bedroom. Sadie followed us, obviously glad that we'd decided to retire for the evening, since that meant she could curl up on her blanket at the foot of the bed and bunk down with her people for the night.

And really, after doing all my nighttime prep, it was closer to nine than eight-thirty by the time I settled myself under the covers. For most of my life, I'd been someone who shifted positions in bed as it suited me, but now I was pretty much stuck with sleeping on my back.

Which was fine. Calvin reached out to take my hand, and I closed my eyes, glad of his touch, glad of his nearness. Even if the baby came tonight, he would be there to handle things, and that was what counted most.

A breath or two, and sleep claimed me.

Next to my ear, my phone was shrilling. Or at least, it sounded shrill, even though my current ringtone was the opening bars of the "Spring" movement from Vivaldi's *The Four Seasons* and shouldn't have been shrill at all.

I jolted awake, laboriously forcing myself to a sitting position. Next to me, Calvin sat up as well.

"What time is it?"

I grabbed my phone and looked down at the screen.

"Twelve fifty-two."

But once I got past the time, I made myself

focus on the number. After all, no one called at that hour unless it was extremely important.

At first, I didn't recognize the phone number. But then my sleep-addled brain saw it was from the 818 area code, which meant it could only be one of three people I knew well, and I sort of doubted that either my mother or Tom would be calling me this late.

"Chloe?" I said as I accepted the call and pressed the phone to my ear.

A terrible little gasp, and then she said, "S-Selena? I didn't know who else to call—"

"It's okay," I told her, even as I felt rather than saw Calvin's body go tense. "What's the matter?"

"It's—" She sucked in some more air in another of those shocked little gasps, then went on, "It's Jack."

"Who's Jack?" I asked.

"M-my boyfriend," she said, then made an odd little sound, almost like a hiccup. "I mean, my ex-boyfriend. We broke up right before I left California."

Not so strange if she was planning to start over in Globe. Except....

"Did he follow you here? Did he threaten you?"

"N-no. I mean, yeah, he came here, I guess. But...."

The word trailed off, and I made myself wait.

She sounded far more upset than a simple argument should have made her, but I didn't know the circumstances. Some people didn't do well in confrontations.

Another breath, and then Chloe said, "I just found him dead in the living room."

Chapter 6

HIT THE ROAD, JACK

By this point, Henry Lewis and I had been embroiled in so many murder investigations that he looked more resigned than anything as he stood there in the living room of Hazel's Airbnb. Chloe was huddled into a corner of the flowered couch, and mercifully, several of his deputies and the EMTs on the scene had already removed Jack's body to a waiting ambulance. Several more deputies were moving around the house, dusting for fingerprints and looking for whatever evidence they could find, which probably wouldn't be very much. According to Chloe, she hadn't even known Jack was here until she left the main bedroom to get herself a glass of water.

"So, you were asleep the whole time?" Henry inquired. Mixed with the resignation on his face was a bit of annoyance, probably at having to drag himself out of bed and come over here in the middle of the night.

Not that I could blame him. Then again, it was probably asking a bit much to request that any criminals in the area restrict their activities to normal business hours.

Chloe nodded. She'd asked me to sit on the couch next to her, but it seemed as though she didn't want any more contact than that, because, after a brief hand squeeze as I seated myself, she'd wrapped her arms around herself as if to stay warm, even though the room was comfortable enough.

"Yes," she said. Her voice shook, and I could tell she was doing her best to hold back tears, since she kept blinking. "I got back from dinner with Selena and Calvin and her parents a little after eight-thirty, and then I watched some TV and went to bed around ten."

"You locked up after you got here?" Henry asked, and off to one side, Calvin shifted his weight from one foot to another. He hadn't said much since getting to the house and obviously wanted Globe's police chief to understand that he was here for me and Chloe, and not because he intended to interfere in any way.

Another nod. "I checked both the front and the back doors, and all the windows were closed because it wasn't warm enough to keep them open."

That was for sure. The days were just beginning to warm a little, but at this elevation, it would be months before the nights were comfortable enough to leave any windows open to catch a breeze.

"I'm not sure if the windows were locked, though," she added, now looking worried. "This is my first night here, so I don't know how everything works."

Henry made a few notes on the yellow pad he held. I often wondered if he even bothered to consult those notes after he wrote them down, since it seemed to me that his memory was just fine for keeping track of the details of a case. For all I knew, that yellow pad wasn't much more than a prop.

"So, you went to sleep, but then you woke up. Did you hear a noise?"

Her teeth tugged at her lower lip. Looking at her now, with her long hair pulled into a scrunchie and not a speck of makeup on her face, I thought she appeared barely old enough to drive, let alone have graduated from college.

"I don't know," she said after a pause. "I just woke up sometime after midnight. For a couple of minutes, I tried to go back to sleep, but then I realized I was thirsty and wanted to get a drink of water. Since I didn't know the house very well, I flipped on the light in the living room on my way to the kitchen. And then—"

She stopped there, but I had a feeling everyone listening knew exactly what was going through her mind.

And then she'd seen her ex-boyfriend's body lying on the rug, and had panicked and called me.

Or rather, she'd done what I guessed a lot of people would have done, which was to reach out to the person she knew best in town rather than calling the police right away.

Obviously, as soon as I'd calmed her down enough to get a quasi-coherent story out of her, I'd told her I'd contact the authorities and that she should sit tight and not touch anything. When Calvin and I arrived at the house, the police were already there, since they had a much shorter distance to cover.

But as far as I could tell, Henry had waited for Calvin and me to get there, apparently thinking it would be better for Chloe to have a few familiar faces nearby while he conducted his interrogation.

Not that what he was doing could be called that, precisely. It seemed to me he was going pretty easy on my little sister, probably because she didn't look like the sort of person who would kill a fly, let alone a human being.

"Was there any sign of forced entry?" I asked Henry, partly because I really did want to know the answer, and partly because it was obvious that Chloe needed a minute or two to collect herself.

His mouth tightened a little. Was he annoyed at me for questioning him?

Well, if he was irritated, it wouldn't be the first time.

However, his tone was civil enough as he replied, "Not that we were able to tell. But I suppose the lock could have been picked by someone who knew what they were doing."

I glanced over at Chloe, and she immediately shook her head. "Jack doesn't...didn't...know how to pick locks."

Henry looked singularly unconvinced. "Are you sure about that?"

She unwrapped her arms from around herself and instead clasped them in her lap. "I don't know. I mean, I suppose it's possible he was hiding that kind of thing from me, but I don't see how. We'd been dating for the past two years. We didn't have a lot of secrets."

A very neutral, "I see," and Henry made another note on his yellow pad. Then he said, "Did Jack Speros know you were here in Globe?"

So, that was Jack's last name. Chloe hadn't mentioned it in her panicked phone call, but I supposed that was one of the first things Henry had asked her after arriving at the Airbnb.

Her lips pressed together. "No. I just told him I

was going to Arizona for a while to figure some things out. We'd already broken up by then, but he kept bugging me to get back together. That was when I said I was leaving California. I definitely didn't say I was coming to Globe, though."

Which begged the question of how Jack Speros could have tracked Chloe down here. Unless....

"Did you ever say anything about me to him?" I asked, and her shoulders lifted, something about the movement heavy, as though she'd had to exert more effort than usual for the shrug.

"I told him I had an older half-sister that I'd never met," Chloe replied. "But when I told him that, I didn't know where you lived, either. So it's not like he would have been able to follow me here based on anything I said back before we broke up."

Strange. To the casual observer, there really wasn't anything to connect Chloe to me—we didn't share the same last name, didn't have a single thing in common except our biological father.

So how in the world was Jack Speros able to figure out where Chloe was staying? Yes, she'd told him she was coming to Arizona, but it was a big state...and Globe was only a very small corner of it.

Judging by the frown Henry wore, he was just as mystified by the situation as I was.

"Do you think Jack could have followed you?" Calvin put in. Even though he'd been doing his best to stay out of the conversation, it seemed obvious that he thought it necessary to ask the question.

"No," Chloe said, and then her fingers tightened on themselves where they sat in her lap. "Or at least, I don't see how. I mean, he drives a big black pickup truck, and I know I would have noticed if something like that was following me all the way from Northridge."

"Maybe he rented a car," I suggested, and a worried flicker went through her slate-colored eyes.

"Maybe," she allowed. "But I was paying attention, and I didn't notice any one particular car following me. If nothing else, they would've had to get off the freeway when I exited to get gas in Goodyear, and I didn't see anyone tailing me to that gas station."

Which seemed to put us back to square one... unless Chloe wasn't telling us the entire truth. Or rather, while she thought she might have been paying strict attention to the road, I could see how she might have been distracted, worried about showing up on her long-lost sister's doorstep, her mind somewhere other than the stretch of highway immediately surrounding her.

I wanted to accept that scenario, since otherwise, I couldn't come up with a single plausible explanation for Jack Speros's presence in Globe.

Clearly, the silence that followed her monologue didn't sit well with her, because she sent me an imploring look and said, "I know he didn't follow me!"

"And I believe you," I said calmly.

One of Henry's eyebrows lifted, but he didn't bother to contradict me.

"Well, let's leave that aside for now," Calvin said, also in the kind of easygoing tones designed to lower the temperature in the room. "Did Jack have any enemies?"

I allowed myself the briefest glance in Chief Lewis's direction. His lips might have tightened imperceptibly, but it didn't seem as though he intended to tell Calvin to butt out. Right then, he was probably just glad to have someone talking to Chloe whom she seemed to trust.

Her brows lifted, not in confusion, but in something almost resembling scorn. "He was a college kid. What kind of enemies do you think he would have?"

She had a point there. Once again, I slipped a quick look from underneath my eyelashes to gauge Calvin's reaction, but, like Henry, he'd adopted a general-purpose law enforcement stone face and wasn't giving anything away right then.

"It depends," Henry said, stepping in when he could tell my husband wasn't going to respond right away. "Maybe he owed his drug dealer money. Maybe he was going after some other guy's girl."

Chloe's slate-gray eyes flashed, stark against her pale face. "Jack didn't do drugs."

"That you know of."

She made a disgusted noise. "We were together for two years. I would have known. He barely even drank."

Her tone was so emphatic that even Henry seemed to think better of trying to contradict her. However, that contained reticence didn't prevent him from saying, "But what about any romantic entanglements?"

Once again, her nostrils flared in annoyance, but she sounded measured enough as she said, "We broke up only a couple of weeks ago. I hadn't heard that he'd started seeing anyone else. In fact, he kept texting me and showing up at the house, trying to get back together with me. My dad finally had to tell him to get lost."

Those words certainly didn't paint a portrait of a man who was ready to move on...which again only made me circle back to why on earth anyone would have wanted Jack Speros dead, and who would have been willing to go to such lengths to make sure he was killed in the living room of the Airbnb where his ex-girlfriend was staying.

Henry clicked his pen and stuck it in the breast pocket of his sports jacket, followed by the yellow pad. "Well, I think that's all we need for now, Ms.

Fairfield. I'll follow up with you if I have any more questions."

Chloe blinked. "That's it?"

"For now," Henry repeated, apparently deciding to ignore the astonishment in her tone. "You've had a rough night, so I'll leave you to go back to sleep." His gaze slid toward Calvin. "Mind if I talk to you in private for a moment?"

"Not at all," my husband replied.

A nod, and then the two of them headed outside, presumably to continue their conversation on the front porch. Chloe turned desolate eyes toward me.

"What am I supposed to do now?"

A good question. It didn't seem right to leave her in a strange place after suffering such a shock, so I said, "Well, I think you should come and spend the night at the house with Calvin and me. I know we'd both feel safer having you there rather than here by yourself."

If anything, she looked even paler than before. "You're sure?"

"I'm sure," I told her, making sure I sounded firm and emphatic. "We have a guest room—it's no imposition. After tonight—or whenever you feel up to it—you can decide what you want to do." I paused there, then added, my tone a little softer, "But tomorrow morning you should really call your parents and let them know what's going on."

Her delicate jaw hardened. "They're going to try to make me go back to California."

"Maybe," I said. "But as you've already pointed out, you're an adult and can make your own decisions. Besides, Henry is probably going to want you to stick around in case he thinks of anything else he wants to ask you. All that aside, I just think it's better if you get in touch with your parents. I mean, think what kind of a shock it would be if Henry called them out of the blue for more information."

That argument seemed to have been the right one to deploy, because some of the fight went out of her eyes as my words appeared to sink in. "You're right," she murmured. "I'll call them in the morning after...after I've had a chance to process all this."

I reached over and took her hand, giving it a gentle squeeze. "It's a lot, I know," I said. "And we're all here for you. We'll get through this together."

From somewhere, she summoned a dreary little smile. "Thanks, Selena." But then she shook her head, saying, "I'm sorry to drag you into all this when you've got much more important things to worry about."

And her gaze strayed to my rounded belly.

"It's fine," I told her. "We'll get this straightened out soon enough."

Worried eyes met mine. "You're sure?"

"Absolutely."

I helped Chloe gather things for a stay of a few days at the house, and then Calvin drove us all home. The whole time, he was quiet, which let me know he had some things he wanted to discuss...but only once we were alone.

Which was fine—I got my sister settled in the guest room, and then, even though it was past one o'clock, I didn't turn off the bedside lamp once my husband and I had settled ourselves in bed, but instead turned toward Calvin, gaze inquiring.

"Jack Speros was strangled," he said without preamble. "The medical examiner will have the final word, of course, but it sounds like someone got him with a garrote."

"Seriously?" I blurted. I could have understood being stabbed or even shot, but to be murdered with a weapon that sounded as if it was out of a spy novel...or maybe a Victorian melodrama?

A grim smile touched the corners of Calvin's mouth. "That's what Henry said. I didn't have a chance to look at the body. But it explains why there wasn't any blood on the living room rug."

Right. It was a hand-hooked piece in shades of blue and green and yellow, echoing the colors in the rest of the room. Bright red bloodstains would have been immediately obvious against the close pile, and even though I knew we had much bigger problems to worry about right then, I couldn't help being relieved on Hazel's behalf that the thing wouldn't have to be replaced.

Well, unless she decided it was better to get rid of the rug to eliminate any possibility of bad juju hanging around the cottage.

"Did Henry find the murder weapon?" I asked, and Calvin shook his head.

"No, his deputies searched the place, but they didn't find anything incriminating. They even looked in the trash bins outside—nothing there, either."

It made sense that there wouldn't be anything in the city-provided garbage cans. Chloe had only moved in the day before, and I doubted she would have had enough time to generate the amount of trash that would have required being put outside in the large bins.

"So...now what?" I asked, and Calvin reached out and took my hand.

"We let Henry and his team do their work. In some situations, I'd say a lot hinged on what the medical examiner has to say, but because the cause of death was pretty clear and there weren't any obvious signs of struggle, I don't know whether he's going to dig up all that much. Still, I suppose there's a chance the murderer left a couple of hairs behind, or Jack Speros might have fought back enough to get some DNA evidence under his fingernails. About all we can do is wait and see."

Waiting wasn't something I tended to be very good at, but in this case, I could see why we didn't have many other options. It sure seemed to me that whoever the murderer was, they'd gotten the drop on poor Jack, because it sounded as if he hadn't made sufficient noise to wake up Chloe. I had no idea whether she was a sound sleeper, and yet you'd think if there had been any kind of a struggle, she would have heard something.

"Okay," I said, and leaned over so I could press a kiss against my husband's cheek. "Then we'll wait."

Chloe was understandably subdued the next morning, and I asked her if she wanted to stay at the house rather than go to the store.

"It's a Wednesday, so I know things shouldn't be too busy, even with the sale I'm running," I told her. We were alone in the kitchen, since Calvin had to be at work at eight and had left more than a half-hour earlier.

But she shook her head, even as her hands tightened around the mug of coffee she held. "No,

I think I'd go crazy if I had to be here by myself all day. At least at the shop, I have more things to distract me."

That was about the same answer I would have given if I'd been in a similar situation, so I didn't bother to argue with her. "I understand," I said gently. "But if you change your mind, that's okay, too."

Her jaw set. "No, I won't change my mind."

So we had a light breakfast of toast and yogurt, and a while later, I drove her to Once in a Blue Moon. Her VW was still parked in the driveway of the Airbnb, and I wondered if she should bring it to my store sometime today, just so she wouldn't have to rely on me to ferry her around. When I brought up the topic as she was unlocking the door to the shop, she nodded.

"That's probably a good idea," she said. "I don't want you to think you have to be my chauffeur or anything."

"Well, I don't mind," I replied. "But this way you can come and go on your own without having to rely on me, especially since I have a doctor's appointment tomorrow afternoon that I can't miss."

"Then maybe I should get the car now?" she suggested after sending a quick glance toward the street outside. As I'd expected, it was very quiet in Globe's downtown that particular Wednesday morning, and I knew this was probably the best time for her to run her errand.

"Go ahead," I told her. "I doubt I'll have anyone beating down the door here, and it should only take about fifteen minutes to walk to the Airbnb and then drive back."

She flashed me a quick smile, one that seemed to let me know she was beginning to bounce back from the trauma of the night before. Not that she was over Jack's death, but only that she could begin to see her way through the tragedy.

Only a few minutes after she'd left to fetch her car, Josie came bustling in, face full of questions.

Clearly, the Globe grapevine hadn't failed her.

"Is it true that your sister's boyfriend was murdered in Hazel's Airbnb?"

"Ex-boyfriend," I corrected her, but Josie, as usual, brushed that fine detail aside.

"Still," she said. "How terrible!"

"It is," I agreed. "I asked Chloe if she wanted to stay home today, but she was adamant about coming into work. I suppose she just wanted something to distract her."

Josie's expression turned solicitous. "I can understand that. What an awful shock, even if they weren't together anymore. Does Henry have any leads?"

"Not that I know of," I said. "But you know he

doesn't share all the details of his investigations with me."

"Well, he should," Josie returned, now looking indignant on my behalf. "After all, you have a much better track record at solving murders than he does."

I smothered a smile and did my best to look suitably serious. "Calvin says we have to wait and see what the medical examiner has to say."

As I'd hoped, that comment neatly deflected Josie from any ruminations on Henry Lewis's and my relative competence at solving murders. "Why, was it poison?"

"No, Jack Speros was strangled," I replied. "But there could still be some physical evidence that wasn't immediately apparent at the crime scene."

Josie gave a serious nod. "I can see that. But where is Chloe? You said she came in to work today, but I don't see her."

"She went to get her car from Hazel's Airbnb. It's not a long walk, and at least this way she'll have her own wheels just in case, even though she's staying with Calvin and me for a couple of days until the shock begins to wear off."

That last comment made Josie take in my oversized belly, and she nodded again. "Yes, this isn't a time when you'd want someone dependent on you to drive them around. Of all the terrible timing!"

I agreed mentally that the situation wasn't

what you could call optimal, but at the same time, I wanted to do my best to gloss things over so Josie wouldn't think matters were any more dire than they already were.

"We'll get past it," I said lightly. "I think the most important thing is to just keep on keeping on, and hope that Henry can get to the bottom of this sooner rather than later."

"I suppose so," Josie said, although I could tell from the dubious note in her voice that she wasn't very confident in our police chief's ability to track down the murderer.

Well, I had to admit I wasn't exactly sanguine, either, but since it seemed clear that he didn't suspect Chloe of the crime, it appeared the best thing to do was wait all this out.

"Anyhow," Josie went on briskly, "I just wanted to check to see how you were doing. I have a zoning meeting I need to get to. Just drop me a note if you need anything."

I assured her I would, and she headed out, moving briskly past the shop's picture window in the direction of City Hall. Once she was out of eyeshot, though, I allowed myself a sigh. While there was no need for me to get involved in this whole mess...well, other than providing Chloe all the support and reassurance she required...I also wasn't sure whether Henry was going to make much headway with this one. How could he, when it seemed as if there was absolutely no evidence pointing toward the killer?

Because my sister came into the shop only a moment or two after Josie had departed, I did my best to keep any doubts I harbored from revealing themselves in my expression. Instead, I asked her how everything went, and she just shrugged.

"It was fine. Actually, it felt good to walk. And now the car's parked out back, so I don't have to worry about that anymore." She paused there and sent me an inquiring glance. "Are you sure you're okay with me staying at your place? Because I really can go back to the Airbnb—I'll just burn some sage and light some white candles to cleanse the place, maybe do a salt ritual."

That was pretty much the same thing I would have done in her situation, even though I hadn't detected any trace of Jack Speros's spirit lingering in the space. Some people might have thought that was all a bunch of woo-woo. However, because I'd interacted with several spirits after their murders, I knew I was fully capable of performing such a feat...as long as the spirits in question were ready to talk.

But it felt to me as though Jack's soul was long gone, and it probably wouldn't be a bad idea to banish any negative energies that might want to hang around the Airbnb. Even if it wasn't haunted, it could still use a decent cleansing.

"Let's see how you feel about everything tomorrow," I said. "Right now, I still think it's better if you're with family."

Chloe's face brightened at my comment, telling me she was happy to hear that I already considered her to be part of my family even if we'd never met before this week. "Sounds like a plan."

She'd barely finished speaking before Henry entered the store, looking grim. Dispensing with any greetings, he looked over at Chloe and said, "Why'd you move your car?"

Her eyes widened a little at his brusque tone. "Selena and I thought it would be better for me to have the car on hand while I was staying at her house. Is there a problem?"

The tight set of his jaw didn't change. "There shouldn't be...as long as you're okay with me checking the trunk."

A nervous glance in my direction, and I gave my sister a very small nod. While I supposed we could have protested and asked for a warrant, I didn't see the point in making trouble. Most likely, Henry had decided an inspection of Chloe's car was necessary, even though he could have had his deputies handle that task the night before.

Maybe he'd spent all morning stewing over the complete lack of evidence in the case and had realized the one place he hadn't looked was inside her vehicle.

"It's out back," she said. "Let me show you."

And while I hesitated for a moment, wondering whether I should leave the front of the shop unattended, I decided it was better to be with Chloe right now. If someone wanted to waltz in and help themselves to a couple of Tarot decks or a few pocket crystals, I wouldn't lose much sleep over it.

Instead, I followed the police chief and my younger sister out to the parking lot at the rear of the building. I didn't see Victoria's red Mercedes SUV and recalled that she'd told me she'd be in Phoenix for most of the day, visiting suppliers and collecting samples from some tile and stone showrooms.

But there was Chloe's dark gray VW Beetle, now starting to get dusty after sitting outside for the past couple of nights, and a few spaces away was my Jeep Renegade.

Henry didn't spare a glance for the Renegade and instead went straight for the VW.

"Unlock it, please," he said.

She pulled the fob out of her jean jacket pocket —I guessed she had stowed it there after she dropped the car off back here—and touched the button to click the lock. Henry stepped forward, pulled on a pair of rubber gloves, and then opened the door and stuck his head inside.

Once again, Chloe sent me a questioning look,

but all I could do was shrug and hope she knew the best thing to do was stand back and let Henry continue with his inspection.

Luckily, it was a pleasant day, the sun out but definitely not hot, the breeze cool without being uncomfortable. Under other circumstances, I wouldn't have minded standing out there while he worked, but after a couple of minutes, my feet started to remind me that I was supposed to be sitting down as much as possible these days, not hanging around in a parking lot while the local police chief conducted what I knew was an entirely futile investigation.

After looking through the glove compartment and under the front and back seats, he backed his way out of the car, eyes narrowed in annoyance. However, his voice sounded even enough as he said, "Pop the trunk."

Once again, Chloe clicked the key fob, and the trunk unlatched and opened a few inches. Henry made his way over there and began rummaging around...and then went very still. Mouth tightening, he reached into the trunk and pulled out a thin piece of wire with a wooden handle dangling at each end.

"Want to tell me what this is?"

Chapter 7

FLYING BY WIRE

"It's not mine!" Chloe protested. "I've never seen that thing before in my life!"

After Henry discovered the garrote in her VW's trunk, the three of us had adjourned to the stock room at the back of the shop. Not sure how long this was going to take, I'd hurried to the front of the store to lock the door and put the "be back at" sign in the window, then waddled back to the cramped space where the police chief had decided to continue his investigation.

"Then what was it doing in your trunk?" he asked, a reasonable enough question.

"I don't know," she said, worry and bewilderment clear in her expression. "But if someone was able to get into my Airbnb without my noticing, then that same person might have been able to get into my car and plant evidence, don't you think?"

Henry's face had never looked sourer. "It's possible," he said grudgingly. "But it's also possible that there wasn't any sign of forced entry because you're the one who killed Jack Speros. Afterward, you hid the murder weapon in the trunk of your vehicle, thinking you'd have plenty of time to dispose of it, especially since neither I nor my deputies looked in there the night of the murder. That's really why you moved your car, isn't it? You thought you'd be able to toss the garrote in the dumpster behind the building here and that no one would ever find it."

True, there was a dumpster out back; Victoria and Archie and I split the cost of the disposal service three ways, since none of us generated enough trash to merit having one for each of our businesses. However, I doubted Chloe even knew it was there, because she simply hadn't been working at the store long enough to take a load of junk out to the dumpster.

I tried to tell Henry as much, and he only lifted an eyebrow as though he couldn't believe I was that naïve.

"You really think she showed up on your doorstep the other day without doing some research first?"

"I *did,*" Chloe said, now sounding justifiably indignant. "I'd never been in Globe before Monday afternoon, and I certainly wasn't driving around looking for dumpsters to throw out hypothetical murder weapons. Like I told you, someone planted that thing in my trunk."

"Maybe so," Henry responded. "Or maybe not. I suppose that's for someone other than me to decide." He paused there, hand resting on the handcuffs that hung from his belt under his sport coat. "In the meantime, though, I'll have to arrest you for the murder of Jack Speros."

Idly, I had to wonder if the Globe police had any plans to place a plaque on the wall behind this particular chair in the station's waiting room. I'd spent enough time there over the past couple of years that I thought it deserved some kind of commemoration.

I wasn't alone in the waiting room, of course—Calvin had come as soon as I called him, and my mother and Tom had hurried over as well. And although I hadn't had a chance to talk to Chloe directly, I'd heard from Loretta Stillman, the deputy who worked at the reception desk in the station, that Chloe had called her parents in California and that they were flying out to Globe as we spoke.

Well, flying to Phoenix, where they'd have to

rent a car. The drive from the airport would probably take longer than the flight itself.

And even though maintaining Chloe's innocence was paramount in my mind, I couldn't help wondering how a meeting between the Fairfields and my mother was going to go. More than thirty years might have passed since she met Jordan in that club in Reseda, but some situations were just awkward no matter how long ago they might have occurred.

Right now, we were waiting to hear what kind of bail the judge was going to require. I had to believe he would let Chloe out on bail, just because —well, as far as I knew, anyway—she didn't have any priors and, while Henry might have found a garrote in her trunk, that evidence was still circumstantial unless they were able to find actual physical telltales on the wire to prove that it had been used to murder Jack Speros.

Still, we were talking about murder here, so I doubted the judge would ask for a ten-thousand-dollar bond and call it a day. Not that it mattered, because I knew I'd pay whatever it took to ensure that my sister wasn't stuck behind bars while awaiting trial.

In fact, Loretta got a phone call, nodded, and then came over to the waiting area. "The judge agreed to bail," she said. "It's $500,000."

My mother might have flinched a little, while

both Tom and Calvin remained impassive. Everyone knew I could handle that amount without any problem, but still, it was a chunk of change...especially since I'd be posting bail for a girl I hadn't even met before a few days ago.

The whole time, Loretta had been looking at me, since she knew I'd be the one putting up the money, just as I had for Calvin and Archie when they'd gotten accused of murders they had nothing to do with. Most likely, Tom could have posted Chloe's bail as well—I never pried into his and my mother's finances, but since they'd paid cash for the big Victorian mansion at the edge of town and I knew he pitched in for his kids' high-flying lifestyles, they were probably sitting on millions as well.

Not that I would ever ask them to help out with my half-sister's bail. My mother had been remarkably cool about the situation, and yet I guessed that might have been crossing a line.

I moved to get up from my seat, and Calvin was immediately there, a helping hand under one elbow. "I'll go with you," he said.

Of course he'd always be there for me. I sent him a smile, and the two of us went over to the cashier's window. Luckily, the amount of money I kept in my various accounts meant I didn't have to worry about getting a bondsman to put up the majority of the cash. No, I just got my checkbook out of my purse, and with a certain air of inevitability, wrote out a check for the entire half-million.

"Thanks," Loretta said, since she often did double duty at the station, both working at reception and accepting payment for whatever fines and fees the citizens of Globe might have incurred with the police department.

Somehow I doubted she would ever see bigger checks than the ones I'd written in the recent past.

With that business handled, though, it meant Calvin and I needed to go back and wait with my mother and Tom, since there was still paperwork for Chloe that needed to be processed. With some effort, I lowered myself back to the chair where I'd been sitting previously, and my mother looked at me with concerned eyes.

"How are you doing, Selena?"

"I'm fine," I assured her, while Calvin sat down next to me. "My passenger has been kicking up a storm lately, but I haven't seen any signs that he or she intends to make an early appearance."

"Good," she murmured, although she still appeared worried.

Well, I couldn't really blame her. Having your only daughter expecting her first child was a momentous enough event without having to factor in an unforeseen murder everyone expected her to solve.

Or at least, I assumed that was what most

people who'd heard of Jack Speros's death must be thinking. And even though I guessed Chloe would never come right out and ask me to help, I knew we didn't have any real alternatives. Relying on Henry didn't seem like a wise idea, because the bare facts of history already told me I had a better chance of fixing this than he did.

Of course, it would have helped if I had a single lead to go on. From what Chloe had told me, it didn't sound as if Jack had any real enemies.

So why would someone follow him to Globe and kill him in the Airbnb where his ex-girlfriend was staying?

I didn't have a clue...literally.

Chloe emerged from the back of the station then, looking a little pale but otherwise composed. Loretta was with her, although she seemed cheerful enough as she said, "She needs to stay in Globe, but otherwise, the judge hasn't put any restrictions on her movements."

Some people might have said that having to stay in my adopted hometown with its population of barely seven thousand people was restrictive enough, but I thought I understood. If the judge had truly wanted to be a hard-ass, he could have given my little sister house arrest, either at my and Calvin's place or at Hazel's Airbnb.

Such harsh measures apparently hadn't been necessary, though, which was something.

"Thanks, Loretta," I said. "Then I think we'll all head home."

She nodded, and all of us got up from our seats —with Calvin steadying me once again—and headed out to our cars. Once we were in the parking lot, though, I looked over at Chloe.

"Do you know where your parents are heading?"

"To the Best Western," she said. Her delicate features were still pale, but otherwise, she looked calm enough.

"That's not a very good place for a meeting," my mother put in, her tone firm. "We should all gather at Tom's and my house."

This invitation made me blink. "Are you sure?" I asked.

Meaning, *Are you really okay with having my biological father and your husband in the same room?*

It seemed she was, because she said, "Of course I'm sure. We'll have the most space there. Also, it's closer than your house."

Well, that was true. The living room at the cozy adobe home I shared with Calvin was big enough for everyone, but we lived a good ten minutes farther outside town at the end of a gravel road that wasn't exactly friendly to regular passenger cars. The Victorian mansion my mother and Tom used as a vacation home was also located at the edge of

Globe, true, and yet it was still much easier to get to.

I glanced over at Chloe. "Do you think they'll be okay with that?"

"Sure," she said, although something at the edges of her voice seemed a bit shaky, as if the word was a little more emphatic than her actual view of the situation. However, she got her phone out of her purse, adding, "What's the address?"

My mother supplied it to her, and Chloe typed out a quick text and waited for a moment.

Then her phone binged, and she said, sounding relieved, "They're fine with meeting at Elizabeth and Tom's house. My mom says they landed about fifteen minutes ago and just picked up their rental car, so they should be here in about an hour and a half."

"Just in time for a late lunch," my mother said. Her expression was far cheerier than it should have been, given the situation, but I had a feeling that was because she was just relieved to have something concrete to focus on, and throwing together an impromptu midday meal for seven people was exactly what she needed to distract her right then.

Which was fine by me. My quiet life might have been upended once again, but the baby I was carrying just wanted to make sure I kept both of us well-fed.

Henry hadn't impounded Chloe's VW—it seemed he'd realized he'd found the one piece of useful evidence in it, after searching the entire trunk and dusting it for fingerprints—so she reclaimed it from the parking lot behind the shop and then joined our little caravan, with Tom's Porsche Cayenne in the lead, followed by Calvin and me in my Renegade, and the Bug bringing up the rear.

Tom pulled into the garage once we got to the property, while Calvin parked the Renegade off to one side in an open space nearby and Chloe did the same. Soon enough, we were all trooping into the house.

"I have lemonade and tea," my mother said. "Do you think we should order from Olamendi's or Cloud Coffee?"

"Cloud Coffee," I replied promptly. "Sandwiches will probably last better if it turns out that Chloe's parents run late, for whatever reason."

My mother agreed that sounded like a good idea, and after consulting with Chloe as to her parents' sandwich preferences and getting orders from the rest of us, she got her car keys out of her purse.

"I thought I'd go to Walmart and grab some fresh fruit and salads as well," she said. "You all don't mind if I leave you alone here for a bit, do you?"

Although it would probably be a little awkward to have her gone, I knew it made more sense for her to do the shopping. She could have given Tom a list, I supposed, but she had a much better idea of what was available at our local Super Walmart and could get the errand handled far more efficiently.

"No, we don't mind," Tom said, and gave her a quick kiss on the cheek. "We'll hold down the fort while you're gone."

She gave him a grateful smile, promised that she'd be as fast as she could, and then headed back out. Those of us left behind glanced around the group, suddenly awkward.

"Well, I can get all your drink orders while we're waiting," Tom said, clearly realizing he needed to play host. "Who wants lemonade, and who wants tea?"

Since I was doing my best to avoid caffeine, I asked for some lemonade, while both Chloe and Calvin requested tea. Tom headed off to the kitchen, and the three of us who remained went to settle ourselves in the sitting room.

"Is this seriously their house?" Chloe asked, looking around in awe. She'd seemed sort of tongue-tied when we first arrived, but now that

Tom was safely in the kitchen, it appeared she was ready to talk again.

"One of their houses," I said. "They bought it a few years ago for a vacation place. Usually, they'll come to town a couple of times a year, but with the baby almost here, they're planning on staying for a few months."

My sister's eyes were still practically owlish. "A house like this, and they barely live in it?"

About all I could do was shrug. "Tom's work keeps him in California a lot, but they fell in love with the house and wanted to buy it anyway, even though it wasn't going to be a full-time residence for them."

This explanation seemed to satisfy Chloe's curiosity, because she gave a nod, even as she continued to look around, taking in all the antiques and the meticulously preserved Victorian architecture. Although I had to admit it wasn't really my style—I liked home decor that was much more easygoing and relaxed—the house was still gorgeous, with its shining wood floors, stained-glass windows, and magnificent staircase and elaborately carved balustrade. The furniture had come with the place, giving it the feeling of a residence that had been almost frozen in time.

Well, except for the kitchen, which had been updated recently and was state-of-the-art.

However, you couldn't see the kitchen from where we sat.

Tom came back a moment later with a silver tray laden with our various drinks. After parceling them out to everyone, he sat down at the edge of the prim couch that was a mate to the one where Calvin and I were sitting—Chloe had taken the armchair off to one side—and said, "I'm very sorry for your loss, Chloe."

She appeared almost taken aback, as though she'd been so absorbed in dealing with her arrest and its aftermath that she'd almost forgotten the reason why she'd been taken into custody in the first place.

"Thank you," she murmured after an awkward pause. "I guess I'm just trying to get my head wrapped around all this. It doesn't feel real, you know?"

Tom nodded, although I wasn't sure whether he really did know. The only time tragedy like this had intruded in his own life was when he'd come here to Globe and had it thrust upon him.

But even when paranormal investigator Brant Thoreau had died on the very staircase located a few yards away from where we currently sat, it wasn't as though Tom had lost anyone close to him. It had been a tragedy, but once the murderer was discovered and everything had been wrapped up in a neat little bow, he'd been able to get on with his life without too much trouble.

Whereas Chloe had lost someone who'd been part of her world for two years. Yes, the two of them had split up, but still, the impact of Jack Speros's loss was probably going to remain with her for a very long time.

Especially if I couldn't figure out who in the world would have done such a terrible thing.

I sent her a sympathetic glance, although she wasn't sitting close enough that I could reach over and give her hand a reassuring squeeze.

"It's hard," I said. "But we'll get to the bottom of this."

"We will?" she responded, her voice quavering a bit on the second word.

Poor kid. It had been hard enough for me to handle being suspected of Lucien Dumond's murder back in the day, when at least I'd been a grown adult managing on my own for years.

How would I have dealt with it if I'd only been barely more than a kid like my little sister?

I honestly couldn't say. All things considered, I thought she was holding it together pretty well.

"Absolutely," I said, my tone firm. Next to me, Calvin shifted in his seat just the tiniest bit, but I knew he wouldn't speak up, not when it was someone related to me by blood who was now in trouble. Otherwise, he might have gently done his best to remind me that our first child was due to appear in less than two weeks and that maybe this was the sort of occasion where I should hang back and let the experts handle things. "We'll wait for your parents to get here and talk everything over, but after that, I'll try to gather whatever evidence I can."

"But there isn't any evidence," Chloe said, her voice and expression both glum. "Or at least, nothing except that garrote thing that Chief Lewis found in my trunk. I still have no idea how it got there."

"Well, that's something we can work on together," I told her, doing my best to sound confident and unruffled, even though I was anything but. "Just because it might look incriminating on the surface doesn't mean there might not be a perfectly logical explanation for why that garrote ended up there."

"Cars are easier to break into than a lot of people think," Calvin put in, speaking for the first time. "Especially car trunks. It makes sense to me that someone got into yours specifically to put that incriminating evidence there. Did Henry find any fingerprints on the garrote's handles?"

She shook her head. "No. Of course, he said I could have just been wearing gloves, but I think that's part of the reason why the judge gave me bail

—there's circumstantial evidence and not a whole lot more."

That new bit of information sounded encouraging. Lacking any real evidence, I doubted the county's case against Chloe would hold up. Still, much better to get her exonerated long before any of this went to court.

"Did your parents say anything to you about an attorney?" Calvin asked then, and she shook her head.

"Not exactly. I mean, they said they'd need to hire someone local but they'd wait to talk to you since you'd have a much better idea of who to approach."

Yes, choosing a defense attorney for your daughter wasn't exactly the sort of thing you wanted to do on the fly with a simple Google search.

"It's not a problem," I told her. "We'll be able to find someone for you...if it even comes to that."

"I'm pretty sure Alec Scurlock will take it on," Calvin said, and I felt my eyes widen slightly.

"I thought he only worked on cases connected with the tribe."

"No," my husband replied. "That is, work for the San Ramon Apache and our indigenous groups around the area makes up the bulk of his caseload, but he takes on outside cases if they're interesting to him. I'll give him a call after we talk to Chloe's parents. I'd want them to sign off first before I reach out to him."

That sounded like a sensible way to approach the problem. Chloe nodded, saying, "I'm sure they'll be fine with whoever you choose. We don't know anyone in the area."

And that was one of the awful things about this whole mess. No, my little sister wasn't on her own, not when she had Calvin and me and my mother and Tom to support her—not to mention her parents—but she was still in unfamiliar territory, wouldn't be surrounded by the kind of support system she would have had if Jack's murder had occurred in Southern California.

For all I knew, that was part of the reason the killing had taken place here.

As soon as the thought crossed my mind, I wanted to dismiss it. Why on earth would anyone need to make sure that Jack Speros was murdered specifically in Globe, of all places? It didn't make any sense.

But then, none of this did.

Calvin talked a little more about Alec Scurlock, explaining how the attorney had defended him when he was a suspect in Dillon James' tabloid-titillating death, and how he'd been on contract with the San Ramon Apache for almost ten years now. I could almost see my sister relaxing as my husband spoke, letting her know she'd be in very good hands...if her parents agreed that hiring Alec was the smartest thing to do.

I reached over and touched my husband's hand, not much more than a brush of my thumb against his, letting him know how much I appreciated the way he was doing his best to reassure Chloe, to let her know we'd all be with her every step of the way. At the same time, though, I couldn't quite keep my thoughts from rattling along, poking at the little I knew about Jack Speros's death.

Why here? Why now? Was Chloe a mark, or an innocent bystander?

I needed to find out why someone would want to do such a thing to Jack...and, by extension, to her.

My mother returned then, laden with so many bags that I wondered if she planned to feed the entire gang dinner and breakfast as well. Tom excused himself to help her with her purchases, leaving Calvin and Chloe and me alone in the sitting room.

"I'm really sorry about all this," Chloe said then, and I blinked at her.

"You have nothing to apologize for," I said, fixing her with a steady gaze so she'd know I wasn't going to allow her to argue with me about this. "We know you had nothing to do with Jack's death, and we're going to do whatever we must to prove that."

Her lips parted as if she wanted to protest, but then she closed her mouth again, apparently realizing I was in no mood for arguments right then.

Just as well, because my mother and Tom came back in with the rest of her shopping bags, and there was some cheerful chaos for a while as she got the dining room set up for our group and Chloe and Calvin volunteered to go into the kitchen and cut up fruit and help with some other meal prep.

Leaving me alone in the sitting room, but that was fine. These days, I was used to being left to sit while the more mobile members of my party went on with their work.

Then the doorbell rang. Since I was much closer to the door than everyone else, I pushed myself to my feet and waddled over to open it.

Standing on the porch was a tall man in his fifties with graying dark hair, and at his side stood a woman I guessed was probably a few years younger, plump and pretty, blonde and with striking gray eyes nearly the same shade as her daughter's.

Now that the moment had come, I found myself almost dizzy.

Or maybe I'd just stood up too quickly.

Despite my disorientation, I managed to find a smile and slap it on my face.

"Hi, there," I said, marveling a little at how normal I sounded. "Come on in."

Chapter 8

READY OR NOT

Jordan Fairfield also seemed to handle the moment fairly well. He returned my smile, then said, “Hi, Selena. This is my wife Heather.”

Since she was looking a little uncertain…it was probably hard enough to be confronted by your partner’s long-lost biological child, let alone one who looked like she was about to give birth at any moment…I immediately extended a hand. “Hi, Heather. I’m Selena. Come on in.”

I stepped out of the way—a lot out of the way, as my distended belly took up so much space—and let them into the house. Judging by the way they glanced around at the museum-perfect interior with widened eyes they were doing their best to hide, I had to guess they hadn’t been inside too many houses like this.

Which was fair enough. There were some gorgeous historic homes in Southern California, but I didn't think many of them were located in the San Fernando Valley.

As we were moving toward the sitting room, Chloe came out of the kitchen and hurried over to her parents. They wrapped their arms around her, asking if she was okay, apologizing for not getting here quickly enough.

She disentangled herself from them just enough to say, "You couldn't have gotten here any faster than you did. And it's okay—I had Selena and Calvin and Elizabeth and Tom to help me through all this."

Almost as though her saying their names out loud had summoned them, the rest of the group emerged from the kitchen as well.

"Hey," I said, figuring I might as well make the introductions now and, with any luck, steamroller over any awkwardness that might have wanted to crop up. "These are Chloe's parents, Jordan and Heather Fairfield. Heather, Jordan, this is my husband Calvin Standingbear, and my mom Elizabeth and her husband Tom McGill."

Somewhere in the back of my mind, I couldn't help wondering if my mother's and Jordan's eyes were going to meet and they were going to exchange some kind of significant glance, the sort of thing that in a film would have been accompanied by hushed chords or at least a bit of slow motion.

This was real life, though, and more than thirty years had passed since the last time they'd seen each other. Both of the involved parties wore a smile that looked pretty natural, all things considered, and it seemed to me they were both just fine with how their lives had turned out.

"Thank you so much for being here for Chloe," Heather said.

"Oh, it's the least we could do," my mother replied, while Calvin and Tom stood a little ways away and appeared glad that at least we'd gotten past the introductions. "Come into the dining room—I have some lunch set out for us, since I figured the important thing to do was for all of us to keep our strength up while we get this straightened out."

Everyone seemed relieved to have food to focus on, so we all trooped into the dining room and took our various spots around the table. As host, Tom sat at the head with my mother on his left, and I sat next to her with Calvin on my left. Jordan seated himself at the foot of the table, and Chloe placed herself next to him, with her mother taking the chair at her daughter's right.

For a few minutes, we were all busy with getting everyone the sandwich of their choice and passing around the bowl of fruit and the pitchers of iced tea and lemonade, but eventually, the food and drink had been handed out and it was time to get down to business.

Jordan sent his daughter a searching look. "So...you didn't have to post bail, Chloe?"

Oops. While I'd known this subject was going to come up eventually, I didn't think it would be the first thing broached during our meeting. Chloe looked over at me and I gave her a nod, letting her know it was okay to provide her father with a straight answer.

After all, that particular detail would have come out eventually anyway.

"Selena paid my bail," Chloe said, and Jordan's eyes widened.

"We would have done that—" he began.

I shook my head and interjected as gently as I could, "I know. But then Chloe would have had to wait even longer in jail, and we thought the best thing to do was to get her out of there as quickly as we could."

Jordan's mouth tightened a bit. It was harder than I thought not to stare at him, to try to see the little details in his face that had come down to me, even though I resembled my mother's side of the family a lot more.

Those telltales existed, though...something about the lift of his brows and even that slight quirk at the corner of his lips. Not a lot, not anything that most people would probably have noticed.

I noticed, though. Not that I'd ever doubted it, but still, sitting there at the table with him told me in no uncertain terms that Jordan Fairfield was definitely my biological father.

But he was Chloe's father, too, and she needed him a hell of a lot more than I did.

"It's nothing to worry about," Calvin said in his deep, calming tones. "Selena will get that money back just as soon as we prove Chloe's innocence."

For some reason, neither Jordan nor Heather appeared particularly encouraged by his words. After exchanging a troubled glance with her husband, Heather said, "But how are you going to be able to do that? I mean, we all know Chloe had nothing to do with this terrible mess, but convincing the authorities may be a whole different story."

No one spoke for a moment, although I noted the way Calvin and my mother and Tom all slipped sideways looks in my direction, as though they felt it was my place to speak since I was the only amateur sleuth sitting at the table.

All right, then.

"Chloe might not have had a chance to tell you this," I said. "But I've had a lot of luck over the past few years solving various murder mysteries around town. I'm feeling pretty confident that I'll be able to get to the bottom of this one as well."

Oh, boy...that sounded way too cocky, especially since I was feeling anything but sure of myself at the moment. At least my track record spoke for itself...mostly.

Once again, Heather and Jordan looked at each other. I didn't know them well enough to catch all their shifts in expression, but I could tell they were sharing the sort of nonverbal shorthand that only a couple who'd been together a long time could usually manage.

"I wasn't aware you were a detective, Selena," Jordan said. "Last I heard, you were a psychic or something, right?"

"Or something," I agreed. "And it's not like I'm a professional private investigator or anything. I just discovered that I have a gift for figuring out mysteries. Some of it may have to do with being psychic."

To my surprise, Heather Fairfield didn't seem put off by any of this. "Like Chloe."

"Yes," I said. Maybe the jury was still out on Chloe's particular gifts—if she had prophetic dreams, why hadn't her sixth sense signaled her that trouble was on the way?—but she certainly believed she had talents in that area, and so, it seemed, did her mother. "That's probably why I've been able to solve so many crimes. It's amazing what a good session with your Tarot cards or pendulum can do for you."

I decided it was better not to mention how the spirit of my Grandma Ellen had also helped me out on several occasions. Reading a Tarot card was one thing; communing with the dead might have been just a bit much for the Fairfields.

Heather reached for her neglected sandwich and took a bite. Then she said, "So...how do you plan to approach Chloe's case?"

"I'm not sure yet," I said frankly. "But probably the first thing I need to look into is Jack Speros's past."

Jordan, who'd just eaten a slice of strawberry, frowned...even as I thought I detected a hint of amusement in his eyes, eyes that were blue but a few shades lighter than mine. "The kid was twenty-two years old. I doubt he had much of a past."

Next to her father, Chloe rolled her eyes, but I could tell she wasn't going to contradict him.

Not when so much was riding on all this.

Calvin spoke up then. "You might be surprised," he said. "I'm not saying we've had to deal with the same problems here in Globe that they have in the big city, but one thing I know for sure is that people can get in trouble at any age."

Since those words were so patently true, no one at the table bothered to contradict him. An uncomfortable silence fell, one that Chloe appeared to think she should fill, since she said, "I'll be interested to see what Selena finds out. All the time I was with Jack, he seemed like a straight-up guy. The only reason we broke up is that he started to get way too clingy...kept talking about wanting to get married even though he hadn't even graduated yet. It started to feel kind of weird."

If the startled expressions on Jordan's and Heather's faces were any indication, this was the first they'd heard about any of that.

"He asked you to marry him?" Heather asked.

Apparently realizing that she might have opened a whole new can of worms, Chloe replied, "Well, not in so many words. It's more that he wouldn't stop bringing up what it would be like to be married, and what kind of plans we should be making for our future. At first, I thought it was kind of cute, because most people our age aren't ready to settle down yet. But then when he wouldn't give it up, I finally pushed back and told him I didn't have any intention of getting married until I was at least twenty-eight or twenty-nine. I mean, who wants to get tied down that young?"

Since I hadn't tied the knot until I was past thirty, I could agree with my little sister's opinion on the matter. Circumstances were different for everyone, of course, but it just made sense to me that she would want to grow into herself more as a person before she leaped into committing to a partner for the rest of her life.

"Well, I'm glad you told him to back off," Jordan said. "Neither one of you was in any position to get into a serious long-term relationship."

His tone was flat, and I had to wonder if he was thinking about the way he'd hooked up with my mother all those years ago. True, they'd used protection, but nothing was infallible.

What would have happened if he'd tried to "do the right thing" and asked her to marry him?

I'd actually asked her that question on several occasions, and she'd always shaken her head and told me there was no way she was going to force him to be with her just because biology had found a way, as it often did. She'd always been emphatic about raising me on her own...and she'd done a damn good job of it.

However, that didn't mean she might not have harbored her own doubts from time to time, trying to decide if she'd made the right choice, especially on those tough days right before the next paycheck when mac and cheese often appeared on the kitchen table and I'd caught glimpses of her going over the bills on my way to brush my teeth, her blonde head drooping a little as she tried to make what was owed to the electric company and the gas company and the cable match up with what remained in her checking account.

"I know, Dad," Chloe said, now sounding annoyed. "And that's a big reason why I broke up with Jack." She stopped there, teeth catching on her lower lip in the now-familiar worried gesture. "But now I can't stop thinking that he would be alive if I hadn't bailed on him and come to Arizona."

"You don't know that, honey," Heather responded at once as she reached over to give her daughter a reassuring pat on the arm. "The problem is, none of us knows much of anything right now."

No, we didn't. And although neither Heather nor Jordan gave me a significant glance, I had to believe they weren't entirely sure I'd be able to pull this off.

Well, that made three of us.

However, the rest of the meal didn't present any hiccups, and it ended with Calvin once again promising to reach out to Alec Scurlock to see if he was available to take Chloe's case. Heather and Jordan wanted to have her go back to their hotel with them, and she agreed, albeit with some reluctance.

"But I'll come back to the house when I'm done," she told me as we made our way down the porch steps, and at once, Jordan lifted an eyebrow.

"You're staying with Selena?"

"It seemed the best thing to do for now," I replied. It still felt kind of strange to interact with him as though he hadn't been out of my life for the entirety of my existence, to act as if this was all perfectly normal. "Neither Calvin nor I thought it was a good idea for Chloe to be alone at the Airbnb so soon after...." I let the words trail off, mostly because there wasn't an easy way to say, *So soon after someone was murdered there.* However, I made myself go on, "But I don't think Chloe has made a final decision as to where she wants to end up. We're just taking it day by day right now."

"Exactly," she said. Then her expression clouded. "Maybe Hazel won't even want me to come back after what happened at her place."

I knew Hazel would never kick Chloe out—especially because she'd texted me earlier that day to tell me she was horrified after finding out about Jack's murder from Henry Lewis, and that she supported my sister in whatever she wanted to do, whether it was to continue her stay at the Airbnb or find someplace else to crash while she was here in Globe.

"You don't need to worry about that," I said gently. "Hazel let me know that she's on board with whatever you decide. It's up to you."

Hearing those words, Chloe sent me a grateful look, telling me I'd eased at least one worry that had been preying on her mind.

Whether I'd be able to help with any of the others was up for debate.

Calvin was quiet as we pulled out of the long gravel drive and onto the street that would lead us back to Highway 60. Once we were cruising along at fifty miles per hour, though, he said, "Do you want to talk about it?"

"Talk about what?" I said absently. My mind had already started picking at the details of Jack Speros's murder, trying to see if it could come up with anything halfway worthy, and I hadn't been paying much attention to my surroundings.

"About meeting your father for the first time."

"Oh, that."

Calvin was in profile to me, but I could still see one corner of his mouth lift slightly. "Yes, that."

I pulled at the seatbelt so it wasn't tugging quite so tightly across my distended belly, then shook my head. "I don't really know what I should say," I replied. "It's like...I saw things in his face that I've seen in mine, and yet the whole situation didn't feel quite real. I mean, I know that Jordan

Fairfield is my biological father, but we still didn't have any connection."

My husband let go of the steering wheel so he could reach over and take my left hand in his right. Feeling his warm, strong fingers against mine helped to dispel some of the air of unreality that seemed to have descended on me from the first minute when Jordan's eyes met mine.

"I think I can understand that," Calvin said. "He's never been a part of your life. There's no reason to think you'd have some kind of immediate rapport."

"But I did with Chloe," I argued. "It's like we clicked from almost the first moment we met."

No immediate response, partly because we were turning onto the gravel lane that led to the house, and he had to slow down and pay attention to the road, still muddy in places from a storm we'd had over the weekend. "It must be very different connecting with someone who's your sister, though," he said. "You've told me before how it would have been nice to have siblings."

Yes, I had. It wasn't exactly that I was jealous of Calvin's large family, but more that I saw something in their interactions that I'd never been able to experience in my own life. And there had also been the way I'd known I had a brother and sister out there but had always been told there was no way I'd ever be able to meet them.

Having a sister show up on my doorstep had fulfilled a dream I'd held deep inside for a long time. It was probably part of the same longing that had made me look at Archie as the brother I'd never had growing up...even while I had to recognize that sometimes he could be a royal pain in the rear.

Even so, I wanted him to always be a part of my life.

"I think it's going to take me a while to process all of it," I said after a long pause. "Honestly, after the horror stories I've heard about other people's families, I suppose I should be glad that our reunion didn't turn into something out of *Jerry Springer.*"

Now the faint lift that had been playing around the corners of Calvin's mouth turned into an outright grin. "You're probably right about that."

Gravel lane turned into gravel drive as we pulled up to the garage and parked. I was silent as he got out of the Durango and came around to my side of the vehicle to help me out. Even a few weeks ago, I might have protested that I was fine and didn't need the assistance. Now, though, I was only glad for about the millionth time that I was going through all this with Calvin Standingbear at my side.

We made our way to the front door and headed

into the house. At once, Sadie came running up to us, tail wagging, while at the same time, her reproachful eyes told us exactly what she thought about us disappearing together like this. Under normal circumstances, she was used to the way we'd both head off to work for most of the day, but with the two of us returning home at the same time, she obviously thought we'd been off doing something fun involving walks and treats and maybe burgers.

"Nothing like that, little girl," I said, while Calvin bent down to fondle her ears. Before I was roughly the size of a humpback whale, I would have leaned over to give her some love, too. Now, though, I knew risking that sort of maneuver might land me flat on my face. "But we'll get you a treat to say we're sorry."

At the word "treat," she went running off toward the kitchen, while my husband and I followed at a slightly more sedate pace. Luckily, the treats were located on a shelf in the pantry at roughly waist level, so I didn't have to do anything more than pluck one out and hand it to Calvin so he could once again lean down to give it to the dog.

With Sadie taken care of, he fetched water for us. My mother's lemonade was very good, tangy and not overly sweet, but I still wanted to clear my palate.

"Are you going to be okay here by yourself?"

Calvin asked as I settled myself on the couch. "I told the guys at the station that I didn't know how long I was going to be gone, but if I head back now, I can still get in a couple of hours."

Guilt over pulling him away washed over me, even though none of this was my fault. Still, I knew Calvin had been doing his best to put in all his regular hours before he went on parental leave at the end of the week, and having him rush off to support me while my newfound sister got bailed out had definitely thrown a monkey wrench into those good intentions.

"I'll be fine," I replied at once. "The sign in the shop window says the store won't be open until ten tomorrow morning, so that part's handled. I'm sure the news has gone all over town already, which means I don't have to waste a lot of time explaining myself."

About all Calvin could do was give a rueful shake of his head. Since he was a native of Globe's environs, if not the town itself, he knew even better than I did how effective its gossip grapevine was.

"I'll only be ten minutes away—" he began, and I had to stop myself from rolling my eyes.

"I'm fine," I said firmly. "No signs of early labor, nothing to tell me this baby isn't okay with sitting it out and waiting for the appointed day. Go on into work—I'll be here when you get back, waiting with my feet up."

He obviously could tell that I didn't want to be coddled, so he just bent down and gave me a quick kiss, told Sadie to keep an eye on me, and then headed outside.

As soon as the door shut, I wondered if I'd made a mistake in shooing him out. The house felt almost too empty with Calvin gone, although I told myself that was silly. I had Sadie here with me, and in a few hours, he'd come home and we'd put together something simple to eat. Back before it started getting harder for me to bend and lift in the kitchen, I'd gone kind of crazy for a week or two, putting together dishes that would be easy to freeze and reheat—soups, stews, all kinds of sauces. Right now both the freezer in the house and the big one in the garage were filled with enough stuff to keep us fed for at least the next three months, so finding something for tonight wouldn't be too difficult.

In fact, that was what I should do now—go into the kitchen, decide about dinner, and then head back to the couch and find something interesting to fill the next couple of hours. Lately, I'd been spending far too much time watching home-improvement shows, but they were mindless and mostly entertaining, and I'd even picked up a few tips I thought I'd put to use when it came time to do something with the spare room.

I pushed myself up from the sofa and winced as

the baby landed a kick in what felt like my lowest rib on the right-hand side.

Feels like I've got a future David Beckham in there, I thought, and allowed myself a smile that wasn't much more than a grimace.

However, since by then I was used to the unending soccer match in my midsection, I ignored the discomfort and went down the short hall to the kitchen. However, I'd only just opened the freezer to inspect the carefully labeled Ziplock bags inside when my phone rang from my purse.

I'd left it on the counter, so I only had to move about a foot to reach into it and pull out the phone. The number wasn't one I recognized, but since it had an 818 area code like Chloe's, I assumed the caller must be one of her parents.

"Hello?"

Heather's voice, sounding rushed, urgent. "Selena, we need you and Calvin to come over. Jack's parents just turned up out of the blue."

Chapter 9

STRAINED RELATIONS

Jack Speros's parents looked as though they were maybe a few years younger than Jordan and Heather Fairfield, although right then, they were emanating such a muddled mixture of anger and grief that it was hard to get a good read on them, except to note that they were both tall and athletic-looking, with his mother sporting a blonde longish bob and her husband dark in contrast, his skin a deep tan that I guessed was a year-round kind of thing.

I'd called Calvin and told him to meet me at the Best Western, then had rushed out...well, waddled quickly...to my Jeep so I could hurry over here.

To say my arrival wasn't exactly welcomed by the Speroses might have been a slight understatement.

"Who the hell are you?" Jack's father

demanded almost as soon as Jordan opened the door.

"I'm Selena Marx," I said, doing my best to keep my tone even. "I'm Chloe's half-sister."

"And she's helping us figure out who killed Jack," Chloe added. She was sitting on the farther of the two queen beds in the room, face pinched with worry, as she and her mother held hands.

Jack's father gave me a disbelieving look. "You're a cop?"

"No," I said. "But I've solved quite a few murders, Mr....?"

I let the words trail off and gave him a direct look, since no one in the room seemed too inclined to make introductions.

"Max Speros," he said, his tone curt. "And this is my wife Leslie."

Saying it was very nice to meet them didn't seem like the right thing to do, so I settled for giving him a nod of acknowledgment.

"Anyway," he went on, "I don't think we need to look any further than this room to see who killed my son."

At once, Chloe sat up a little straighter, hot color burning high on her cheekbones, bright in her otherwise pale face. "I didn't kill Jack. That's what I've been trying to tell you."

"Well, of course you would say that," Leslie Speros put in, her voice just as tightly wound as her husband's. "And I'm sure you'll get a jury to believe you, with that innocent face of yours."

"Okay, okay," I said, holding up a hand. "I know tempers are high, and rightly so. But let's look at this logically. Why in the world would Chloe have a motive to murder your son?"

Leslie's chin lifted. "Because he dumped her, and she couldn't take it."

My eyes widened, and Chloe wore a similarly owl-eyed look.

"*I* dumped *him,*" she snapped.

Rather than look offended, the Speroses shared a glance that bordered on smug. "Well, of course that's the story you spread to everyone," Max said. "But we know what our son told us."

"Which wasn't the truth," Jordan shot back. "He obviously wanted to misrepresent what really happened because he didn't want to admit that Chloe broke up with him."

"That is not—" Leslie began, but didn't get any farther than that, as someone knocked at the door right then.

Jordan, who was the one who'd let me in the hotel room and who'd remained standing near the door, went ahead and opened it. Outside stood Calvin, wearing his tan San Ramon tribal police uniform.

"You called the cops on us?" Max demanded.

"No, he didn't," Calvin said calmly as he came

inside. "I'm not here in an official capacity. I'm Calvin Standingbear, Selena's husband. It sounded like she needed some moral support."

The Speroses went quiet then, clearly unsure as to how they should proceed. True, my husband had just said he wasn't here in his role as chief of the tribal police, but still, he was such an imposing figure in his uniform, six and a half feet tall and with waist-length black hair pulled back into its usual Navajo silver clasp, that his mere presence had clearly cowed them a bit.

"I did need some moral support," I said, going over to him so I could slip my hand in his. Then I looked at the Speroses. More than anything, I wished I could see their auras, but it didn't seem as if those shimmers of telltale color intended to make an appearance any time soon.

So I'd just have to rely on gut instinct. I honestly didn't think they were bad people but were trying to find a scapegoat, trying to find an easy solution to their son's death when they didn't know what else to do. And since Chloe had already been arrested for Jack's murder, it felt as though they'd latched on to her as the obvious suspect because that was easier than sitting back and waiting for the police to produce another possible killer.

"This is a tragedy all around," I said, still trying my best to sound calm and soothing, doing whatever I could to cool the temperature in the room. "You've suffered a terrible loss. But I know Chloe had nothing to do with Jack's death."

Leslie Speros sniffed. "Of course you'd say that —you don't want your little sister to go to prison."

"No, she doesn't," Calvin said. "Because Chloe's not guilty. I think the best thing for everyone involved is to take a step back and allow each other some space. That means going on back to your own hotel or wherever you're staying."

"It's an Airbnb," Max Speros said. His voice still had that hard note in it, but I could tell he'd already taken Calvin's measure and knew there was no way he'd emerge the victor in a physical confrontation with my husband.

And that didn't even take into account the obvious problems involved in assaulting an officer of the law.

"Your Airbnb, then," Calvin replied, still sounding completely unruffled.

Max Speros looked at his wife. Her mouth tightened a little, but otherwise, she didn't reply.

However, even that small response seemed to be enough for him, because he gave her a brusque nod, and then the two of them walked out of the hotel room.

The door slam as they left was enough to make me wince.

"Thank you," Jordan said. "I tried to tell them

that confronting us here wasn't a good idea, but they wouldn't listen to reason."

"I've never seen them like that before," Chloe added. Her voice wasn't much more than a whisper, and she cleared her throat before she went on, "They were always so nice to me."

"Well, people often show their true faces when they're under a lot of stress," I told her. "And I can understand why they're not acting completely rational right now. But at least it seems they've come to their senses enough to realize they need to respect your boundaries."

"A guy in a uniform can have that effect," Jordan observed, his tone now dry. With the Speroses gone, he seemed much more relaxed.

Not all the way, though. I had a feeling the tension in his shoulders and the taut look to his jaw wouldn't disappear completely until his daughter had been exonerated.

"Glad I could help," Calvin said, although a frown pulled at his brows. "What I can't figure out is how they knew to find you here."

"That's my fault," Heather replied. She pressed her lips together, guilt clearly tugging at her. "I thought it would help Leslie to know where we were staying so we could meet after they got to Globe. I never in a million years thought they might actually believe Chloe was responsible for Jack's death."

On the surface, it seemed a strange conclusion to leap to, especially when Chloe had been in their son's life for several years and would have had ample reason to off him if she truly did have murder on her mind.

But people often liked to latch onto the closest target, and if Jack truly had lied to them and said that he was the one to initiate the breakup and not vice versa, I could see why they might have viewed her as a woman scorned, someone who wanted to get rid of the person who'd caused her so much pain.

Of course, that didn't explain why Jack had come to Globe if he was the one who'd walked away from Chloe. However, I had a feeling his parents would find some way to justify his actions, even if they didn't make much sense at first glance.

"I'll let Henry Lewis know what happened here," Calvin said. "Things didn't get too out of hand, but still, he should be aware that the Speroses are openly hostile to your family and may do something rash. I have a feeling that if they know the local police are keeping an eye on them, they'll behave themselves a little better."

Thank the Goddess for Calvin. I knew he'd present the situation factually, with zero embellishments, but at the same time, he'd also make Henry aware the Speroses were something of a wild card.

Or loose cannons.

"We appreciate that," Jordan said. He reached up to push a hand through his gray-flecked hair, hair that was probably almost as thick as it had been back when he'd met my mother in that club in Reseda. "But I'm also sorry for dragging you into all this. Heather called because we didn't know what else to do."

"It's fine," I replied, then looked over at Calvin. He didn't appear too worried by the situation, which told me he knew the Speroses were going to be on their best behavior for at least the next little while. "Honestly, I was just sitting at home, trying to figure out what to defrost for dinner. This was much more interesting."

Both of Chloe's parents chuckled then, and she got up from the bed so she could come over and give me a quick hug. "You are seriously the best big sister in the world," she declared.

"I don't know about that," I said. This time, my cheeks were the ones that were flushed. "But I'm glad—we're both glad that we could help."

"So...what should we do now?" Heather asked. Unlike her husband, she was still obviously upset by the encounter with the Speroses, her face pale and her voice shaky. "I mean, this is a pretty small town—no offense. I don't know how we're supposed to keep avoiding them for however long all this is going to take."

Chloe turned back toward her mother. "Mom,

I already told you that I don't expect you to stay here the whole time. We don't even know how long it's going to take to get a trial date. You know you and Dad can't stay away from your jobs that long."

Heather's mouth set. "We're not going to abandon you—"

"It's not abandoning her," I cut in, but gently. "Calvin and I will be here for her—and my mother, too. She was already planning to be here for at least the next three months, maybe longer. You don't have to worry about Chloe not having a support system."

While my words seemed to cheer Heather a bit, I couldn't ignore the direct look she gave my rounded belly. "I think you're going to have your hands full very soon," she remarked.

"I am," I said calmly. "But I've got Calvin and his whole family as well as my mom. We'll have attention to spare for Chloe, I promise."

Something about Jordan's expression was almost skeptical, as though he couldn't quite let himself believe that I'd have any energy or time to spare for this newfound sister of mine. To my relief, though, he didn't try to protest, but only said, "And Heather and I really appreciate that."

A smile touched my lips as a thought popped into my mind. "I think I know how to avoid the Speroses...at least for the rest of the day."

It was a good thing I had so much food in the freezer—and that the dining room at Calvin's and my house could accommodate a big group...at least, once we put the leaf in the table.

Of course, Jordan and Heather had tried to demur, pointing out that they could handle themselves if they bumped into the Speroses at one of Globe's few dining establishments. The ranks of those restaurants had swelled slightly over the last couple of months, thanks to Sofia Barnes getting her brewpub up and running in record time, but still, the odds of encountering Jack's family were at least one in four.

It just seemed smarter to have the Fairfields over at the house and avoid running that particular risk.

The weather that day was mild enough that Calvin could take everyone on a hike to use up some time, while I remained at home. As much as I enjoyed hiking around these hills with my husband, I knew I wasn't up for that kind of activity at the moment...and probably not for at least another couple of months.

Instead, I thought I should take advantage of the unexpected free time to consult the Tarot and see if it could provide me with any insights into the true killer's identity. I probably should have done so earlier, but the events of the past couple of days had spilled over me like a river in flood, and this was the first time where it felt as if I had the opportunity to truly calm my mind and allow it to be open to any messages the universe might want to send me.

So I went into my office and lit some white sage incense, the kind that always seemed to create the sort of soothing space I needed for this sort of work. Off from their shelf came my set of beloved Everyday Witch cards, and then I started shuffling.

It took a while before I felt the tingle in my fingers that always told me when it was time to stop and pull a card. In situations like this, I generally liked to pull three; it had been a long time since I'd done the much more elaborate Celtic Cross configuration, mostly because that was the sort of card pull I'd done for clients in the past who'd booked me for a full reading, and I'd left the Celtic Cross behind the same way I'd left the life I'd once lived.

Now, though, I only wanted to get some clarity and—if I was lucky—a few hints that might guide me in the direction I needed to go.

The very first card was the Devil, and a worried breath escaped my lips. True, I was performing a reading to track down a murderer, so I doubted I would pull any truly beneficent cards—like the Star or the Nine of Cups—in a situation like this. But....

Well, at least it's not the Ten of Swords, I told myself with a mental grin. That grim image of a hapless witch lying face-down in the road, her back pierced by ten blades, tended to come up all too often when I was doing these readings.

Then again, this was only the first card in the pull.

Back to what was lying on the altar in front of me. In general, the Devil represented temptation, being swayed from one's true path by giving in to greed or lust or sometimes just taking the easy way out of a difficult situation. Sometimes it could also signify feeling helpless, of being controlled by outside forces. Whatever interpretation was at work here, it wasn't anything positive...which didn't surprise me too much.

The next card was the Seven of Swords reversed, and I let out a hiss of breath from between my teeth. Once again, not something you wanted to see in a personal reading, as it was often connected to deceit or betrayal. I didn't always pay much attention to reversals, letting the overall feel of a reading guide how I was supposed to interpret a card, but in this case, its lesser meaning of keeping secrets might very well be in play.

Question was, who was keeping secrets from whom?

It was way too early to make a definitive judgment one way or another, so I paused for a moment, holding the remaining cards in my hands, praying to the universe and the Goddess to guide me to something that would provide the most illumination.

My fingertips tingled, so I pulled out the card they were touching and laid it on the altar.

The Emperor, reversed.

I frowned, staring down at the trio of cards that lay on my pretty blue and green springtime altar cloth. In many cases, the Emperor was a positive card, but reversed like this, it could indicate some kind of controlling figure, or even a lack of discipline.

But which meaning of the card was at work here?

Put together, the collection of cards didn't seem to have an overall direction. Loss of control. Betrayal. Domination.

But who had felt out of control and dominated? Jack Speros?

Nothing Chloe had told me about her former boyfriend seemed to match that description. All right, possibly he'd felt betrayed when she broke up with him, as though his life was out of control, and yet I had the nagging sense somewhere deep inside that I wasn't reading this set of cards correctly.

Which meant that the best thing for me to do was to leave them lying on my altar for now, so I might go back from time to time and revisit them to try to get a better sense of what they were attempting to tell me. Standing here and frowning down at them wasn't going to change anything.

Besides, my feet hurt.

I left my office and went back to the living room so I could elevate my legs for a while. Calvin and Chloe and her parents had only been gone for about a half hour, so I knew I still had some time alone. The hike he'd taken them on wasn't particularly strenuous—none of them had been dressed for anything more challenging than a glorified walk—but it would still keep them occupied for a good chunk of the afternoon. Then we could have an early dinner, and the Fairfields could go back to their hotel...which I had to hope wasn't being surveilled by the Speroses.

Sadie had followed me out of my office and then jumped on the couch so she could snuggle next to me. My belly was far too big for her to sit in my lap anymore, but she still seemed to be content to just be close like this. I stroked her tiny, silky head and fondled her oversized ears, and she leaned into me, glad of the extra attention.

Then my stomach seemed to clench, and I pulled in a sharp breath.

Was that a contraction?

I sat there, dead still, my hand lying on Sadie's back. For a moment or two, I didn't dare breathe.

What would happen if I went into labor now, with no one around to help me?

You're not going into labor, I told myself. *Dr. Carlisle said you might get a twinge here and there, but it's perfectly normal.*

True...but what if that really *had* been a contraction?

Then you'll call Calvin and you'll call your doctor. He has his phone, and it's not like you're stranded in the middle of the Gobi Desert or something.

As the seconds passed, I realized that the sudden ache in my belly hadn't been anything more than the twinge my doctor had mentioned. All right, "twinge" was sort of downplaying the sensation, but since no others appeared ready to follow, I knew everything was fine.

For now.

I dismissed that thought as best I could. All the same, the unsettling sensation had served as a harsh reminder that this baby was coming soon, and if I didn't do some hard work between now and then, I might not be able to help Chloe clear her name.

Problem was, I didn't even know what form that hard work should take.

Chapter 10

SAGE ADVICE

DINNER WAS QUIET AND PASSED MOSTLY without incident, although Chloe announced that she wanted to go back to her Airbnb after this evening.

"I don't want to keep imposing on you," she told me. "I know you have a lot going on, and I can handle staying there by myself."

Her parents didn't look too pleased by the prospect. "What about the Speroses?" Heather asked. "After the way they acted today, I wouldn't put it past them to pounce on you the second you're alone."

While I didn't want to entertain thoughts of such an unsettling scenario, I had to agree inwardly that Chloe's mother had a point. If nothing else, the Speroses didn't seem to have a very good notion of how to respect other people's boundaries.

However, Chloe only lifted her chin and said, "I don't think they'd do that. They were upset at the hotel, but now they know they were out of line, and I think they'll stay away."

Jordan tapped his fingers against the side of his plate. Being out in the sun and the wind seemed to have done him some good; his face had picked up a little color, and he'd eaten the very basic meal of spaghetti with meat sauce, salad, and garlic bread with a good appetite. However, he couldn't help frowning as he said, "I wish we could petition the judge to let you come back to California. I'd feel a lot better with you there."

But Calvin shook his head, saying, "It's better not to rock the boat. Chloe will be safe here."

"Doubly safe," I put in, "because I'll go with her to the Airbnb tomorrow morning and help her cleanse the place and surround it with some protection energy. No one should bother her after that."

Heather's expression was dubious, to put it mildly. "Do you really think that will work?"

"Mom," Chloe returned, wearing the kind of look that only a daughter thoroughly exasperated with her mother could manage, "Selena knows what she's doing."

She stopped there, but I could practically hear her adding mentally, *Stop embarrassing me!*

Somehow, I managed to keep myself from smiling.

"It's all right," I said. "Most people don't have a lot of experience with this kind of thing."

"We've always allowed Chloe to explore whatever she found interesting," Jordan put in. He'd watched the exchange between mother and daughter without comment, probably because he'd heard that sort of back-and-forth multiple times before. "And it's not that we doubt your talents. But this is our daughter's safety we're talking about here. I think it's understandable that my wife might be concerned about trusting it to a few lit candles and some sage waved around."

At his seat, Calvin shifted, and I could tell he didn't much care for the other man's dismissive tone. However, I'd encountered that kind of attitude plenty of times before in my life—and, no doubt, would meet it countless times in the future—and I wouldn't allow myself to get too ruffled.

"It's true that on the surface it might not seem like a lot," I said. "But you'd be surprised by how changing the energies of a place can ward off people with negative intentions."

"Don't treat me like I'm a kid," Chloe said. "Please."

That last word, uttered quietly and simply, seemed to be what struck home with her parents, because neither of them offered any protests.

"If you think it will work," was all Heather said, and I nodded.

"I'm sure it will."

They left a little past seven, and Calvin and Chloe and I spent the rest of the evening watching a movie. None of us wanted to talk about Jack's murder or all the tumult of the day, although Calvin got a text message midway through the film and smiled.

"Alec Scurlock will take the case," he said. "He apologized for getting back to me so late, but he was out on the Navajo nation all day and didn't have good cell service. He wants to meet with you tomorrow afternoon."

Chloe sent me an uncertain glance. "Don't you have a doctor's appointment tomorrow?"

"I do," I said. "We'll just close the store for a few hours. It's not the end of the world. It's much more important for you to meet with the attorney."

She seemed to see the wisdom in that, because she replied, "Okay," and Calvin sent back a quick text. A moment later, his phone binged again.

"Tomorrow at two," he said. "Alec is going to be here in Globe meeting with the tribal elders anyway, so he'll see you after that. It saves you having to drive to Payson to meet with him, since his office is up there."

Chloe's bewildered expression might have been comical if the situation hadn't been so serious. "Where's Payson?"

"About an hour and a half north of Globe along Highway 188," I said. "It's a pretty drive. But still, much better for you to meet Alec here in town."

With the matter apparently settled, Calvin picked up the remote and started the movie again.

I wanted to relax, but something inside wouldn't quite let me. Yes, Chloe now had a lawyer.

However, I wanted to eliminate the reason for having one at all.

Just like the past couple of days, Calvin had to leave early to be at work at eight. Today, though, Chloe and I also needed to get an early start so we'd have plenty of time to get the Airbnb cleansed before heading over to the shop. We'd need to lock up a little before two, but that would still give us almost four hours of being open, and with the weekend approaching, business should be decent.

We'd driven to the house in separate cars, of course, since Chloe would be coming back here at the end of the day and not to Calvin's and my place. As I parked at the curb, I found myself staring at the Airbnb, and its cheerful yellow paint and flowers just starting to come back to life in the garden beds.

It definitely didn't look like the kind of place that had been the scene of a brutal murder only a couple of days before.

I pulled in a breath, then heaved myself out of the driver's seat before going around to the cargo area of the Jeep so I could get out the bag of supplies I'd brought along. It wasn't all that much, just some white candles and a few bundles of white sage that came directly from the San Ramon reservation, along with a couple of small bottles of moon water.

All I could do now was hope it would be enough.

Chloe met me on the front porch, her expression tense. "I've never done anything like this before," she told me as she unlocked the door.

I tilted my head at her. "I thought you said you'd done cleansings for friends of yours."

A dismissive hand wave, and she said, "That's not the same. It's not like I was dealing with a murder or something."

Well, she had a point there.

"The principles are basically the same," I said.

She still looked dubious, but rather than reply, she pushed the door inward and walked into the house, chin now up in the attitude I now recognized as her way of pushing herself forward even when she wasn't sure of the outcome.

I followed her. Even though I hadn't felt any residue of Jack Speros's presence when I'd been here the night before last, I still tensed, wondering what I would do if he'd decided to take up residence in Hazel's Airbnb after all.

But the space felt curiously neutral to me. Even without a lingering ghost, there still might have been some dregs of the violence enacted here left behind, part of the reason why I'd thought it would be a good idea to perform a thorough cleansing of the place.

However, I couldn't sense a single thing. Henry's deputies had been detailed but also careful, which was why I didn't spy a single knickknack or other item out of place, not even some fingerprint powder left on a surface.

Chloe must have noticed the same things I had, because she said, sounding almost disappointed, "Maybe we don't need to do this after all."

"No, we still should, even if the house seems okay," I replied. "It's always better to take precautions, just in case."

She was quiet for a moment, surveying the flowered couch, the prints that echoed the home's bright colors of blue and green and yellow. Then she nodded, saying, "Well, I told you I wanted to learn from you, so this seems like it would be a good place to start."

"This isn't school," I said, almost amused, and her shoulders lifted.

"Maybe not exactly, but it's still better to work with someone who knows what they're doing, right?"

I supposed she had a point there. While I'd never had any formal training myself, relying mostly on books and then later on, watching some YouTube videos from people who were respected members of the witchy community, I knew that not everyone had the same learning style. For Chloe, it might just be better for her to have an example right in front of her.

"Well," I said, "the first thing we should do is get these white candles set out and lit, and then we can go from there."

I was still holding the bag with all my ritual supplies, so I reached inside and handed one of the pillar candles to her, followed by the long-handled lighter I'd also brought. She set the candle down on the TV stand, which was placed against the eastern wall.

Soon enough, all the candles had been put in positions roughly corresponding to the four cardinal directions. She sent me a questioning look and I said, "Go ahead and light them. As you do so, imagine a sphere of white light surrounding this place and everything inside."

A nod, and she went ahead and lit the candles one by one, even as I murmured, "Goddess, grant us peace and protection within this space."

Once Chloe was done, she came back to me and set the long-tipped lighter down on the coffee table. "Do we smudge now?"

"We won't be smudging at all," I responded. "We'll light the sage and carry it through the house, but that should be enough."

Her expression was a little puzzled. "You don't smudge the traditional way?"

"Sometimes," I said. It seemed clear enough to me that most of what she'd learned had probably been gleaned from YouTube videos and maybe online articles and blogs, and she didn't have a lot of real-life experience. So much of being a witch was about intuition, about going where your instincts and the universe guided you, rather than parroting rituals you'd learned from secondary sources. "I'll do that when I'm moving into a new space, or sometimes if I feel a place's energy has become stagnant. That's not what I'm sensing here, though." I paused there before adding, "Give yourself a moment to become still and absorb the energies of the space. I think you'll see what I mean."

Her brows drew together, and she gave a

thoughtful nod. Then she closed her eyes and spread her arms wide, as though to drink in all the micro-currents in the air that surrounded us.

I held myself as still as I could, even though my feet were already beginning to hurt and I would much rather have made my way over to the couch and sat down. Doing so would have disturbed Chloe's meditation, though, so I told myself this shouldn't take very long and that I needed to be mindful of her process.

To my relief, she opened her eyes a moment later, her face now reflecting a sort of wonder. "You're right," she said. "Why didn't I notice that before?"

"Probably because you haven't had a lot of practice letting yourself simply be," I replied. "Being a witch isn't always about doing. Sometimes it's about stillness."

"Like meditation?"

I tilted my head, considering the question. "Sort of," I said. "And I do meditate, but that's a little different from what you just did now. In this particular situation, it's more a case of letting yourself be open to whatever energies might exist in a space."

"I definitely don't think Jack is here," she told me.

"Neither do I. But it's still good to make sure the place is clear and neutral, and that protections are set up so you don't have to worry about anything hostile coming near the house."

Now her slate-gray eyes were wide, reflecting real fear. "You think whoever killed Jack might come back to get me, too?"

"Not exactly," I replied quickly, since the last thing I wanted was for her to be in a fearful state when we cast the protection spells. It was very important to be in a calm and mindful place when working any kind of magic. "Honestly, I don't really know what we're dealing with here. If it was a personal grudge, then there would be no reason for the murderer to come anywhere close to the scene of the crime. But at the same time, I just think it's smarter to put as much protection in place as possible."

My words seemed to calm her, because the worried look left her eyes, and now she seemed more thoughtful than anything else. "I can see that."

"Good," I said. "Because I think it's important for you to do the protection work."

Once again, her eyes flared with concern. "I don't know how to do that!"

Although I'd never imagined myself as a teacher of the magical arts, I knew I needed to provide some guidance without sounding too pedantic. "This isn't like Harry Potter," I told her, making sure my tone was gentle, calm. "It's not about learning specific spells and repeating them without any thought as to what the words actually mean. This kind of magic is all about intention. We both already know you have the gift, so it's just a matter of channeling it in the direction you choose."

Her expression turned skeptical. "But what about all those people who claim they have spell books and stuff to work their magic?"

Personally—although there were a few gems to be found here and there—I thought that most supposed practitioners of magic on social media were doing it for clicks and views, and not because they had any true talent. In those cases, reciting flashy spells made it seem as if they were accomplishing more than they actually were. Most of the time, I considered them harmless —even annoying specimens like Instagram star and sometime witch Lilith Black, who'd definitely bitten off a lot more than she could chew when she came to Globe to celebrate the solstice and had ended up murdered by one of her assistants—but when someone with an actual gift, like Chloe, tried to emulate them, the results were never good.

"Some people find they work better that way," I replied, doing my best to be diplomatic. "But if both our magic came from the same source—and there's no reason to think it didn't—then it just stands to reason that you'd have more success following my method, right?"

Chloe mulled that possibility for a moment. "I suppose so," she said, and even produced a half-hearted smile. "Maybe I've been making this harder than it needs to be."

"Exactly," I said, knowing I should leave things there and see what happened. "So, take a moment to think about when you've felt the safest, when you knew everything was going to be fine and absolutely nothing bad was going to happen. Then take that feeling and hold it in your mind as you send that same energy to protect this house and everything—and everyone—in it."

She inclined her head toward me, acknowledging those instructions, and then she closed her eyes, face blank with concentration. I held myself still again, knowing that even a small movement might be enough to interrupt her thought processes.

Of course, the baby chose that moment to kick, but I wouldn't let myself react. After all, I'd been putting up with the internal drumbeat for the past five months or so.

Chloe's lips moved, although I couldn't tell exactly what she was saying. Not that it mattered. What mattered was she believed those words were the necessary ones to conjure a blanket of protection that would keep her safe for as long as she stayed in this house.

And even though it was her spell and I had no real hand in it other than giving her some words of advice, I could somehow feel the atmosphere in the room shift, become even calmer, warm in a way that had everything to do with spirit and nothing at all to do with the actual temperature the thermostat was set at.

Then her eyes opened, and her mouth curved in a smile. "It worked."

The word ended on the slightest of upward inflections, as though she was mostly sure she'd gotten the charm of protection right but still needed outside confirmation.

"Yes, it did," I said, smiling as well.

However, she didn't seem quite as at ease as I'd expected, considering how effective the cleansing had turned out to be. Her brows pulled together as she looked around the living room, and she said, "I've been thinking and thinking. You know, about who could have done it."

She stopped there, expression still troubled, and I sent her an inquiring look. "You thought of someone?"

"I don't know," she said. "But when I told you that Jack didn't have any enemies, I might have been wrong. I mean, it all happened before Jack and I even started dating, so...."

"What happened?" I asked.

Chloe fiddled with a fold of her skirt. "I guess during his freshman year at Cal State Northridge, Jack got caught up in some kind of cheating scandal. He didn't do it," she added hastily. "And the school totally exonerated him. But the other kid got kicked out. I heard he ended up having to go to a private college on the East Coast, someplace where his parents could kind of buy his way in."

I wanted to think this was a promising development, but I couldn't be sure. Would someone really hold a grudge that long over an incident that, while embarrassing and inconvenient, might not have turned out to be terribly detrimental in the long run?

Maybe so. For all I knew, the boy who'd been forced to move across the country to escape his shame had discovered his bad reputation had followed him, and that even after several years had passed, he might find it hard to find a job once he graduated.

This was all pure speculation, though.

"Do you remember the other kid's name?" Because even though I guessed this was probably a long shot, it still bore some looking into.

Chloe's small white teeth caught at her lip. "Um...Bryce something."

Well, that wasn't very helpful. "Could you narrow it down a little?"

Despite the tension in her face, she couldn't seem to help flashing a smile. "It was kind of an unusual last name. Bryce...Bryce...." The words trailed off, and then her grin broadened. "Bryce Arsenault."

That name sounded like something out of a historical romance novel. But I had to admit it was a lot more unusual than "John Smith," so I had to hope it wouldn't be too hard to track Bryce down, wherever he'd ended up.

"Perfect," I told my little sister. "I'll have Calvin look into it. And now, we can go to work."

There were no worries about the two of us being at the store, since I did much the same kind of cleansing in my shop every few months or so, just to be safe. True, those precautions couldn't protect me from all mischief—like the rock Kurt Vonn had thrown through my window a few months earlier in an attempt to distract me from discovering who'd killed Trent Reynolds during the holiday brewing competition—but even in that case, the vandalism had occurred in the dead of night while I was miles away at home and safely away from the shattering glass.

And although I'd had a couple of items shoplifted over the years I'd been operating Once in a Blue Moon, I knew that sort of petty crime would have occurred much more often if I hadn't done my best to make the store a safe space.

I settled myself on the stool behind the counter while Chloe went around and tidied up the few books and crystals that needed to be put back in their proper places. She seemed cheerful enough, and I was glad for that. It couldn't be good to have a murder charge hanging over her head, but at the same time, she'd taken a proactive step toward protecting herself back at the Airbnb, and she had her meeting with Alec Scurlock this afternoon to look forward to.

Earlier this morning, while I was in the shower, she'd talked to her parents, and they'd agreed to go back to California on Saturday. As Chloe had already pointed out, it wasn't as if they could stay in Globe indefinitely, and at least by waiting until the weekend, they'd have a chance to sit down with their daughter and her lawyer and get a better idea of where things stood. It sounded as though neither Jordan nor Heather was entirely happy about the prospect but had realized they simply weren't in a position to remain here for months. True, the docket in Gila County moved a lot faster than it did in the Phoenix area because of our much smaller population, but still, if this ended up going to trial, it would take a while.

I couldn't quite ignore the feeling of relief

that came over me when I heard those plans. Yes, we'd all gotten along together better than I'd thought we would, but it was still a little awkward to be around my biological father and his wife.

And things improved even more when I got a text from Josie a few minutes after Chloe unlocked the shop's front door.

I heard that the Speroses are leaving tomorrow. They just wanted to be here to handle having their son's body sent home.

If I hadn't lived in Globe for almost three years by that point, I might have asked Josie how she'd managed to acquire that particular piece of information. However, I knew my friend's data-gathering skills were second only to those of an NSA operative, so I didn't bother. The most likely explanation was that she'd talked to someone in the police department, or maybe someone who worked at the local funeral home, and they'd given her the skinny.

The important thing was that we wouldn't have to worry about encountering the justifiably angry and grieving parents of Chloe's former boyfriend. While my heart ached for them and what they were going through, I also knew they were directing their anger toward the wrong people. Chloe was family—and Jordan and Heather as well, in a slightly uncomfortable sort of way—and I didn't want anyone making their lives any more difficult than they already were.

And if the medical examiner had released Jack's body to be taken back to California, that meant he must have concluded his investigation. I hadn't heard anything about that, but I wasn't exactly on Henry Lewis's email list.

I'd asked Josie what the coroner had found, and even her reply text had sounded slightly annoyed.

I don't know. I've been trying to find out, but no one else in the department seems to know anything, either.

Under other circumstances, this all might have seemed somewhat suspicious, but I had a feeling the reality was much more mundane. Henry wasn't talking because the medical examiner hadn't found anything that didn't line up with the obvious cause of death.

I had to believe that could only be good news for Chloe. If they'd found something incriminating—her fingerprints on the wooden handles of the garrote, or her DNA under Jack's fingernails—then I had to believe Henry would have been in contact with her. Now, though, the evidence was looking more and more circumstantial.

And if that was the case, then it seemed to me the chances were good that her lawyer might be able to make the entire thing go away.

To my surprise, the first person through the

shop's doors that morning was Hazel. We'd been communicating by text so she had something of an idea of what was going on, but it seemed she wanted to talk in person just to reassure herself.

"How are you?" she asked Chloe, who also seemed somewhat startled to have her sort-of landlady show up out of the blue.

"I'm fine," she said. "Selena's been taking good care of me."

"That sounds about right," Hazel replied, a corner of her mouth lifting, as though she hadn't expected to hear anything different. "I just wanted to make sure there wasn't anything else I could do to help you out. I can understand why you might not want to stay at the house after what happened, so I checked with Mavis Jones to see if any of her Airbnbs are available. She's got one free for the rest of this week and next week, too."

At once, Chloe shook her head. "I appreciate you doing that for me, but I'm fine with staying at your place. Selena and I did a cleansing there this morning, and I know it's totally safe."

Only three years of being my best friend probably prevented Hazel from lifting an eyebrow at that comment. While she'd never gotten on board with all the woo-woo stuff, she knew it was important to me...and that, although she had her doubts, she couldn't argue that my methods were pretty effective.

"If you're sure—" Hazel ventured.

"Oh, I'm sure," Chloe said firmly. "It's a darling house, and just because something awful happened there, that doesn't mean I should leave. Besides, I think moving to a different Airbnb would make it seem as if I was feeling guilty about Jack's murder, you know?"

I hadn't thought about it that way, but I could see why Chloe might believe such a thing. Yes, she'd come to stay with Calvin and me for a couple of days to get over the shock of her ex-boyfriend's death, but going away indefinitely might have signaled to some people that she was avoiding the Airbnb because she couldn't bear to be continually reminded of the place where she'd killed him.

Hazel looked somewhat more skeptical, but it seemed she realized she shouldn't argue the point, not when it already appeared as though Chloe had her mind made up.

"Well, I'm glad you decided to stay," Hazel said, her tone studiously neutral. "And you just let me know if there's anything else you need."

"I will," Chloe promised her.

After that, Hazel headed out, saying she needed to stop in the Sundowner Gallery down the street to check on the placement of a new painting she'd dropped off the day before. Once she was gone, I looked back over at my little sister.

"So...you really are going to stay at the Airbnb."

"Well, yeah," she replied. "It would have been kind of silly to go to all that work cleansing and protecting the place if I wasn't going to actually sleep there. Like I said, I don't want to intrude on you and Calvin any more than I already have. It'll be fine."

She looked so confident that I didn't dare contradict her. Besides, she was right—there was absolutely nothing in the house that could hurt her, and all signs seemed to point to this being an isolated incident. I had to believe that Henry was following up on any possible leads, doing his best to discover who in Jack Speros's circle of friends and acquaintances would have been motivated enough to come to tiny Globe, Arizona, to seek his revenge.

Well, except for the part where Chloe had already told me that Jack didn't have any real enemies, except possibly Mr. Bryce Arsenault, erstwhile cheater of tests. I thought then of the card reading I'd done the afternoon before.

The Devil. The Seven of Swords. The Emperor.

Temptation and weakness. Betrayal. A controlling outside force.

What was it supposed to mean?

Right then, I didn't have a clue.

Chapter 11

DISTANT THUNDER

While we had a decent number of patrons that morning and through the lunch hour, I didn't feel the slightest pang as Chloe set the "be back at" sign in the window and locked the front door a few minutes before two.

She, on the other hand, seemed to have some doubts. "I can always come back and open up for an hour or so later this afternoon," she told me as she deposited the key in the cash register. "I don't think the meeting with Mr. Scurlock is going to take much more than an hour."

"Maybe not," I said. "But it could go long, and you and your parents are probably going to have plenty to talk about even after the meeting's over. It's fine."

Another hesitation, but then she seemed to

guess from my expression that I wasn't going to budge on that point.

And I wouldn't. Going over strategies for defending yourself in a murder investigation was a lot more important than a couple of hundred bucks in sales, if that. While business was a bit more brisk than it would have been if I weren't running a half-price sale this week, I'd noticed that it had begun to trail off as the week wore on, telling me the early bargain-hunters had already come and gone. Having the shop closed for a few extra hours wasn't going to make much of a difference.

So Chloe got in her VW and drove off to the Best Western, where Leland Price, the manager, had offered her and her family the meeting room for their talk with Alec Scurlock, and I climbed into my Renegade and navigated the half-mile or so to the OB/GYN's office.

This close to the big day, the check-up was mostly about discussing how I was feeling and taking a few readings to make sure the baby's heart was still beating just fine and that I didn't seem to be in any imminent danger of giving birth on the floor next to one of the bookcases in my shop.

"Everything sounds great," Dr. Carlisle informed me. I'd been expecting exactly that evaluation, but even so, it felt good to hear it coming directly from her lips. "Looks like we're right on schedule."

It was good to know that all the recent hubbub didn't seem to have affected the baby, but I also knew I needed to bring up that little episode the other day, when something that felt dangerously like a contraction had shuddered through my body.

After I described it, though, Dr. Carlisle only shook her head.

"That's perfectly normal," she said. "I know it can be scary, but it's nothing to worry about, especially since it only happened one time." She paused there, gaze sharpening a little. "Are you doing your best to keep off your feet?"

"Mostly," I said with a wry smile, thinking of how long I'd been standing in the living room of the Airbnb while Chloe set her protection spell on the house.

"Well, try to make it more than 'mostly,'" the doctor said. "And you're still planning to close the shop after this week?"

"Not anymore," I replied, then added quickly, "My younger sister is in town, and she's going to keep an eye on things for me while I'm on leave."

I knew all this would be news to Dr. Carlisle, because she was one of those "strictly business" types of people who tended to focus on patient care and not gossip. Very likely, she'd heard nothing about Jack Speros's murder, or the way my long-lost half-sister had appeared in Globe only a few days before the tragedy. We had a local paper, but it only came out once a week, and wasn't due to land on people's doorsteps and driveways for a few more days.

The doctor's expression brightened. "That's good to hear. It's wonderful when family can pitch in after the baby arrives. Then I won't give you my speech about taking sufficient time off both before and after your due date."

"No worries," I assured her. "I'm already planning to be home for at least six months."

"Perfect," she said. "I know not everyone has the luxury to take so much time off work, but if you do, you should take advantage of it."

We ended the appointment with her telling me I really shouldn't drive after this week, and to call the second I had contractions around five minutes apart. Afterward, I went out to my Jeep and climbed in. It felt as though I had even less room between my belly and the steering wheel than I had the day before, even though I had the seat pushed as far back as I reasonably could and still reach the brake and gas pedal.

Well, that was probably why Dr. Carlisle wanted me to stop driving. And I would; after this week, Calvin would be off work, too, and he could play chauffeur while we waited for the baby to arrive.

As I was driving down Bridge Street, I spied

Victoria's red Mercedes SUV approaching from the other direction and lifted my hand to wave. We'd been sort of missing each other the past few days, with me zigging while she was zagging, so it was good to catch even a glimpse of her.

But you'll see her Saturday at brunch, I reminded myself.

Thinking of that rapidly approaching event, I wondered if I should reach out to Heather to see if she might want to delay her and Jordan's departure by a day so she could attend our girls' get-together as well. My mother had already shown that she was fine with hosting Heather Fairfield at her house, and I knew she wouldn't mind if I added another guest to the roster.

Or maybe that would be weird. I could tell things were still sort of awkward with my bio-dad and his wife, and asking her to a baby shower when she'd only met me a few days earlier might seem strange. Not that it was a true baby shower—I'd told everyone I didn't want any gifts—but still.

No, probably better to let it go. It wasn't as if Jordan had been in my life while I was growing up, and I barely knew Heather at all. The baby I was carrying was his grandchild, true, but I didn't see the point in forcing things when we really didn't have a relationship.

The steering wheel jerked in my hands, and I

started from my reverie, wondering if a tire had just blown. But no, I wasn't getting any tire-pressure warnings from the display on my dash. I clamped down on the steering wheel, feeling it shudder against my fingers, as though the tires it was steering were being directed by something other than my own will.

What the hell?

Then it was as if an invisible hand grasped the wheel, turning it hard to the right. I'd already lifted my foot from the gas the second the steering wheel started acting up, and now I frantically reached for the brake with my foot, straining to touch it, cursing myself for pushing the seat so far back. I really hadn't had a choice, but—

The Jeep swerved across the road, straight for an old oak tree that had stood at the corner of Broad Street and Maple for at least fifty years. My foot finally found the brake and I slowed.

Not enough, though.

In the next second, the front end of the Renegade crashed into the tree, and everything turned white as the airbag exploded around me.

"I'm fine," I said irritably, for what felt like the hundredth time.

All right, shaken up, and with some inevitable

bruising where the seatbelt had held me in place during the crash, but I hadn't gone into labor, hadn't seemed to have suffered any real injury except the aforementioned bruises.

Standing next to me, Calvin shook his head. A tight line between his brows signaled his worry, and he looked paler than anyone with his dark-toned complexion ever should. "I knew you shouldn't have been driving this late in the pregnancy."

After the world stopped spinning, I'd dug my cell phone out of my purse and called 9-1-1. The EMTs arrived almost immediately to transport me to the emergency room at Cobre Valley Medical Center. Since Calvin was my contact, they'd called him as well—and Dr. Carlisle, since I'd retained enough presence of mind to let the paramedics know she was my OB/GYN.

Now, after a thorough check-up to ensure the crash hadn't caused havoc with the baby, both the doctor and I were satisfied that I'd escaped relatively unscathed.

Calvin, on the other hand, didn't seem nearly as convinced.

"I cleared her to drive," Dr. Carlisle said crisply. "Yes, I said it was better if someone could be her chauffeur, but many pregnant women can drive right up to their due date. Luckily, Selena had her seat pushed fairly far back, and that was what helped lessen the impact on the baby from the airbags deploying."

Thank the Goddess for that...well, except for the part where I might not have crashed at all if I'd been able to adequately reach the brake pedal.

And what the hell was going on with the steering wheel? Had the mechanism failed? The car was less than two years old, so that scenario didn't seem very likely.

Then again, mechanical failures happened all the time, even on new or almost-new vehicles. We'd have our local mechanic check it out, and if he couldn't find anything, then we'd have the Jeep towed to the dealership in Gilbert where we'd bought it.

"Well, she's not driving anymore," Calvin said, his tone flat.

I might have argued that it wasn't his place to tell me what I could or couldn't do, except I was in whole-hearted agreement with my husband on that point. Although I was fine except for a few bumps and bruises, my hands wouldn't stop shaking, and I didn't think I wanted to get behind the wheel of a car again for a long, long time.

Especially a wheel that had felt as if it was possessed.

An image flashed into my mind of Travis Cox's car after its rollover, right after I came to Globe all those years ago. Someone had put a hex on it, causing him to crash the Subaru he used as the town's single Uber/Lyft driver....

His words from the scene of the accident came back to me.

It's, like, something just grabbed hold of the car and rolled it.

No, my car hadn't rolled, but whatever had taken hold of the wheel had been doing its best to make me crash.

"What is it?" Calvin asked, his expression shifting to one of worry.

I wasn't going to tell him I'd just seen a ghost, because I hadn't. All the same, I couldn't stop thinking about Athene Kappas, Lucien Dumond's right-hand woman. She'd been killed in that rollover because she hadn't been wearing a seatbelt, while Travis had managed to escape with only some bruises on his forehead and a nasty mark on his neck from the very seatbelt that had saved his life.

Because Dr. Carlisle was standing right there, I responded the only way I could.

"We can talk about it when we get home."

A tow truck had already taken the Renegade to the local body shop, so inspecting it would have to wait. Besides, I knew Calvin would never agree to that kind of field trip without getting me home first so I could put my feet up for a while and drink some chamomile tea to calm my nerves.

"All right," he said, once I was settled and he'd fetched me that much-needed cup of tea. "What was it you couldn't talk to me about back at the emergency room?"

"I think someone might have put a hex on my car."

At once, his eyes narrowed, but he knew better than to suggest that scenario was ridiculous, not when he knew such a thing was more than possible.

"Like what happened to Athene Kappas?"

I blew on my tea. Part of my brain didn't want to acknowledge that someone would wish me ill in such a way, but the Renegade had been a perfectly reliable car from the second I bought it. There hadn't been any warning signs that the steering mechanism was starting to go bad, no reason to think anything was wrong with it at all.

"I'm afraid so," I said. "But I need to see the car and feel its vibes to know for sure."

My husband's jaw set almost imperceptibly. Looking at him, most people would have thought he appeared utterly calm, but I knew him better than that.

The merest hint that someone might have been magically gunning for his wife and his unborn child had awakened a quiet, deadly rage. Although

I had no reason to love the person who'd placed that hex on the car, I couldn't help thinking they had no idea what they'd started.

"The same person who killed Jack Speros?" Calvin asked after a long pause.

"Maybe," I said. "I don't have enough clues in hand to know one way or another. But getting a sense of that hex—if there really is one—might be one way to get started."

"All right," he said grimly. "Then drink that tea, and we'll go check it out."

No one at the body shop stopped us from going to look at the Jeep. It sat in a corner of the lot, looking forlorn, the front end completely smashed in.

That had been a very big tree.

"It's all right," Calvin said. He had his arm around my waist and had helped me walk from his Durango to the spot where the Renegade was parked. I hadn't suffered any material hurt from the accident except a few bruises, but I had a feeling the shaky sensation in my legs was going to take a while to go away. "It doesn't look like the frame was bent, so the insurance probably won't total it." A pause and a keen glance from under his straight black brows, and then he added, "Unless you find something here that makes you want to get a new car."

On the surface, that might have been a good idea. However, something stubborn inside me balked at having to buy another vehicle just because some unscrupulous user of magic had meddled with this one. Once it was cleansed and protected, it should be good to go.

As long as Calvin was right and the insurance company didn't declare it a total loss.

"We can worry about that later," I replied, my free hand moving over my rounded belly. "I don't think I'm going to be in any shape for car shopping for a while."

He nodded. "Whatever you want to do."

What I wanted to do was hit "rewind" so the events of the past couple of days had never occurred. All right, that wasn't exactly true. I was very glad Chloe had come into my life, even if she seemed to have inadvertently brought a trail of destruction along with her.

Calvin's steadying hand still on my arm, I went over to the Renegade. We'd told the manager of the body shop that I needed to get a few personal items out of the vehicle, which wasn't even a lie. The EMTs had salvaged my purse from the wreck, but the bag of supplies from the home cleanse Chloe had performed was still sitting in the trunk, along with a few health and beauty odds and ends I'd bought at Walmart a while back and kept forgetting to bring into my house.

At any rate, fetching those items provided all the cover we needed for me to inspect the car and see whether I was merely the victim of bad luck…or a particularly nasty little curse.

I tried to tell myself it had to be the former, just a mechanical failure of some kind. Otherwise, shouldn't I have sensed the hex the moment I approached the vehicle in Dr. Carlisle's parking lot?

Maybe…maybe not. Although I'd felt much more on top of things psychically once I was past the first three or four months of my pregnancy, I couldn't deny that I wasn't operating at peak form, either. Many pregnant women experienced much the same sort of symptoms, except their occasional brain farts didn't affect their psychic powers.

And I had to admit I hadn't been paying much attention. Buoyed by the knowledge that the pregnancy was progressing completely normally and that my child would be here in only a little more than a week, I'd gotten into the car and started for the house, thinking of not much more than putting my feet up and relaxing until Calvin got home.

So it was very possible that I'd missed some warning signs.

However, when I went over to the Jeep and

placed my hand on the hood, I didn't feel a single thing. No warning twinges, no sense of something dark and twisted attached to the vehicle, the way I'd sensed that cloud of cold wrongness surrounding Travis Cox's mangled Subaru all those years ago.

Calvin sent me a questioning look, and I gave him a very small shake of my head.

"Nothing."

"Well, that's only one spot," he said. "Maybe the hex was placed somewhere else on the vehicle."

I knew he was trying to be encouraging, but if someone had crawled under the Jeep and scrawled a dark sigil there, it wasn't as if I could find it in my current shape. If I got down on my hands and knees right now, I kind of doubted I'd get back up again without a crane to assist me.

And although I knew Calvin would cheerfully get under there himself if he thought it would help, he wasn't a witch. Even if someone had scratched a hex mark somewhere on the undercarriage or drive-train, he wouldn't have been able to detect it.

Rather than point that out, I moved toward the back of the Renegade. As soon as I got within about a foot of the license plate, creepy-crawly sensations began running up and down my back.

"I think there's something here," I told my husband. "Do you have a screwdriver with you?"

Basically a rhetorical question, since I knew the

Swiss Army knife he carried on his belt had what felt like a gazillion different attachments. However, since I didn't have them memorized, it wasn't as if I could know for sure.

He pulled the knife out of his pocket and deployed the screwdriver gizmo. A minute or so later, he pried the license plate off the back of the car.

Underneath it, someone had scratched a symbol into the paint, something that looked vaguely like a dagger pointing downward with several loops and crosses near the top. Because I'd never studied dark magic, I had no idea exactly what it was, only that it hadn't been put there to ensure happiness and long life.

"Is that...?" Calvin began, and I nodded.

"It's a sigil of some sort. Clever of them to hide it under the license plate—that's not the kind of place people would generally look unless they're switching out their plates for some reason." I paused there, eyes narrowed as I stared at the evil little symbol. "And I suppose I didn't sense it when I got into the car because I didn't detect anything now until I got pretty close. I just got right in the driver's seat after my doctor's appointment."

My husband's eyes had narrowed, a sure sign he was thinking of all the things he'd like to do to the person who placed that symbol there, if and when we eventually caught up with them. However, his voice sounded even enough as he said, "Who would do something like that to you?"

I shrugged. Not the most eloquent of responses, but I was just as flummoxed as he was. One might have said that I'd racked up my share of enemies over the years, thanks to the way I'd put nearly a dozen murderers behind bars, and yet I couldn't say for sure whether that was what we were dealing with here. The few people who might have wanted revenge on me—for whatever reason—weren't witches. They wouldn't have even known anyone who could have created a sigil like this, let alone scratch it into my car themselves.

"Honestly?" I said. "I have no idea. There isn't anyone in Globe who practices this kind of magic."

Even as I spoke, however, I wondered whether I should be quite so confident on that point. True, there were others here who dabbled in Tarot or other kinds of minor magic, but they weren't true practitioners, simply people who were interested in the occult and wanted to play with it a bit.

Whereas whoever had hidden that sigil under my Jeep's license plate definitely knew what they were doing.

Calvin's grim expression didn't flicker. "From somewhere else, then."

"Maybe," I allowed. "But the only people I ever really knew who dealt in this kind of thing were members of GLANG, and it's been disbanded for years."

"You're sure about that?"

"Sure" might have been an overstatement. On the other hand, I'd kept in touch with Maisie Hoskins, an old friend of mine who was the proprietor of a witchy store in West L.A., and from what she'd told me, it sounded as if the Greater Los Angeles Necromancers' Guild had completely fallen apart after Lucien Dumond's death. Some of its members had tried to start their own little groups, but they didn't seem to have lasted for very long.

"I don't know," I said. "I suppose it's remotely possible that a former member of GLANG might be gunning for me, but why now? They've had years to get their revenge, and yet everything has been completely quiet on that front."

Calvin's lips pressed together. He looked away from me to the mark on the tailgate, then asked, "Is there a way to remove that thing?"

Well, at least I had a ready answer to that question. "Oh, sure," I said. "We just need to scratch it out, and then I can cleanse the spot with moon water and place a spell of protection on the car. It'll be good as new."

Assuming the insurance company didn't total it after all. We'd paid a decent chunk for it, but even

I knew vehicles depreciated like crazy almost the second you drove them off the lot.

My answer seemed to have relieved Calvin at least a little bit, because something in the tense set of his jaw eased. "Good to know," he said. "All the same, I'm just glad this thing is going to be in the shop for a while."

"Same," I responded, doing my best to keep my tone light. "For now, though, let's go home."

Chapter 12

THE STUFF OF NIGHTMARES

ALTHOUGH ABSOLUTELY NOTHING OUT OF the ordinary happened on our drive home from the body shop, I was still on edge enough that I made Calvin remove the Durango's license plate once we were parked in front of the garage, just to make sure the same evildoer hadn't placed a sigil there as well.

But we didn't find anything, despite my walking around the big SUV, fingers trailing across the smooth white paint, looking for something that wasn't there.

"You might as well park it in the garage," I told Calvin. "It's not as if the Jeep is going to be in here for a while. And I'd just feel safer that way."

My husband's eyes narrowed slightly at that request, but he didn't say anything, only got back into the Durango and pulled it into the garage.

Luckily, we'd reclaimed the remote for the opener when we were at the body shop, so managing that task was easy enough.

Once the garage door was shut and we'd gone into the house, some of the tension that had been knotting my jaw and neck seemed to ease just a little. Maybe it had been silly to imagine the unknown worker of dark magic creeping onto our property and casting a hex on Calvin's police-issue SUV, but at the same time, I thought it better to take whatever precautions we could. The house and the land it sat on were protected by the same sorts of spells I placed on my shop, and yet I knew all too well that they weren't foolproof.

As far as I knew, nothing was.

But it did feel good to sit down and put my feet up while Calvin went into the kitchen to get us both some water.

He was barely out of the living room when my phone rang. Since it was inside my purse and I'd set the bag down on the floor next to the sofa, I didn't have to reach very far to pull it out.

Josie, of course.

"Selena!" she exclaimed. "Are you all right? I just got out of a meeting and heard what happened!"

"I'm fine," I told her, even as I allowed myself a slight smile at her words. Well, that explained why she hadn't called me within five minutes of the accident. I did not doubt that if she hadn't been in that meeting, she would have known about my crash right away. "And the baby's fine. Calvin and I are home, and the Jeep's at the repair shop. We don't know yet whether it's totaled."

"How awful! Do you know what happened?"

"I'm not sure," I said, knowing I needed to be circumspect here. It was all fine and well to discuss hexes and sigils with my husband, but Josie still wasn't entirely on board with all the witchy stuff. Better to make it seem as though the accident had a completely mundane cause. "Mechanical failure, maybe. We'll have to wait for the mechanic to look it over and see if he can find anything."

The question was, would such an inspection even reveal anything out of the ordinary? A sigil designed to invite disaster might have worked on the Jeep...or it could have affected me and my handling of the vehicle directly, in which case there really wouldn't be anything mechanical to find. If that turned out to be the case, then I'd have to take the blame for the accident. Most people would probably excuse the mishap by saying I was in a state where I really shouldn't have been driving in the first place, but I doubted my insurance company would see things that way.

Well, I'd deal with that later. Right now, I had bigger things to worry about.

"That's terrible," Josie said. "Isn't the car still under warranty?"

"It is," I replied. "And, like I said, we'll just have to wait and see what the mechanic has to say about what went wrong. But Calvin and I have decided I'm going to stay home after this. I only had one more day to work this week anyway, so I'll just let Chloe take over a little sooner than we'd expected."

Josie didn't reply immediately. Was she trying to think of the most tactful way to say that she wasn't sure I should leave my store in the hands of someone so young and inexperienced, especially one who also happened to have a murder charge hanging over her head?

While my friend wasn't necessarily the most tactful person in the world, she seemed to realize saying something like that when I was already under a lot of stress probably wasn't a very good idea. After that uncomfortable pause, she responded, "Well, it's good that you have Chloe here to watch the store while you're out on leave. Have you talked to her?"

"Not yet," I said. "She and her parents were meeting with Alec Scurlock this afternoon, and I expect she'll call once she has some concrete information to pass along."

"It's good that Alec is on the case," Josie replied at once. "I'm sure he'll be able to make all this go away soon enough."

That was my hope, too, but it was way too early to say for sure. I settled for making a noncommittal sound, then said, "Thanks for the call, Josie, but I'm kind of beat after everything that's happened. I'll see you on Saturday at my mom's house."

"Of course," she said. "You just let me know if you need anything."

I promised her I would, and then I ended the call and set my phone down on the coffee table. Right then, Calvin came into the living room, a glass of ice water in either hand.

"Josie?" he said, and I nodded.

"I'm kind of surprised she didn't call sooner," I told him. "But yes, she just wanted to make sure I was all right."

My husband's expression was almost amused. He gave me one of the glasses of water and then sat down on the armchair next to the couch, probably so he wouldn't jostle me and my poor, abused feet, which were currently propped up on a pillow.

"I'm glad she checked in," he said. "Especially because I know she'll spread the word all over town, and maybe that way, you won't have to field so many phone calls checking to see if you're okay."

I wrinkled my nose, but at the same time, I knew he was right. Once word of the accident made its way around town, I had no doubt I'd be getting a bunch of calls from friends and well-wishers wanting to confirm for themselves that I truly had managed to survive the crash mostly unscathed.

"We'll see," was all I said, and he only smiled.

"The important thing is for you to get as much rest as possible," he told me. "And I also think that I'm going to beg off work tomorrow, too. It's only one day, and I know I'll feel better if I'm here with you rather than at the station."

As much as I would have liked for him to be at my side keeping watch, I didn't know whether those measures were necessary.

"It's perfectly safe here," I pointed out, and I could see the way his jaw set from where I sat.

"Maybe it is," he said. "But we both thought your Jeep was perfectly safe, too, and look how that turned out. Whoever is trying to cause havoc in your life, I don't want to give them any openings. It's much better to play it safe and hope they'll give up once they realize they won't have another chance to try to hex you again."

I reflected that Calvin had come a long way over the past couple of years, or I doubted he would have mentioned hexes in such a casual tone. And he had a point. His deputies would understand why he wanted to be home with me. To tell the truth, it would have looked a lot stranger for him not to stay with his nine-months-pregnant wife after she'd been in such a terrible accident.

"Okay," I said, and set down my glass of ice water so I could reach out and take him by the hand. His fingers were warm and strong and callused, utterly reassuring. That was the hand of the man who'd been at my side for almost the past three years. How could I possibly think it was okay to let him go to work when we had no idea who was lurking out there, just waiting for another chance to create some major havoc in my life?

"I think we're both officially on leave now."

He made a few calls—including one to Ben Ironhorse, a San Ramon tribal police deputy with a knack for hacking databases, just to see if he could discover anything about Bryce Arsenault—while I petted Sadie and pretended to watch TV, and a little while after that, my phone rang.

"Oh, God, Selena, I just heard!" Chloe said, sounding a little breathless and a lot worried. "Josie said you were fine, but—"

"I am," I assured her. "However, Calvin and I think it's better if I stay home until the baby arrives. Are you okay with taking over the store tomorrow?"

"Sure," my sister said stoutly. "Absolutely."

I'd been expecting her to respond just that way, but still, it was good to hear that she didn't sound at all worried about beginning her solo run at the shop a bit earlier than she'd expected. "How did it go with Alec?" I asked.

Although I couldn't see her face, I had to believe her expression shifted at that question. "Oh, great," she said, sounding much more upbeat. "He was very confident that the police don't have much of a case. He's going to file a motion to dismiss tomorrow."

Just the kind of news I'd been hoping to hear. "Still no evidence?"

"None at all," Chloe said cheerfully. "Sure, they found that garrote in my trunk, but it didn't have any fingerprints on it, and they couldn't find any DNA evidence that couldn't have gotten on the thing because of the way it was just dumped in there with my other stuff. So, Alec is pretty sure that when he presents all the evidence to the judge, they'll drop the charges—and you'll get the bail money back."

The cash bond I'd put up for my sister's freedom was the least of my worries right then. However, I could tell she was concerned about it... or maybe it was more that Heather and Jordan didn't like the idea of being so beholden to me. Either way, I wouldn't be sad to have the money returned, even while it meant much more that Chloe had been exonerated.

Unfortunately, I knew some people wouldn't

look at the situation the same way. Having the charges dropped wasn't the same thing as being proven innocent openly in court. Would people whisper behind her back, saying she'd gotten away with murder?

That wasn't a very good way to start a new life in a new town.

I was getting way ahead of myself, though. Alec might have been hopeful that the judge would drop the charges, but until it actually happened, there wasn't much point in wasting time on speculation.

"That's great news," I told her. "And your parents are still planning to head back to California on Saturday?"

"Or maybe Sunday," Chloe replied. "It all depends on what happens with the judge tomorrow. If Alec can get the charges dropped, then they won't have as much reason to stick around." She paused there, as if weighing whether she should say anything else. However, she seemed to decide she should be frank with me, because she added, "Honestly, they're not super-thrilled about me staying here in Globe, even though they know I'm doing it to help you out."

"And I appreciate it," I said at once. If Chloe hadn't come to town, I would have had no choice except to close my store. Now I could take my leave without worrying about what would happen to Once in a Blue Moon.

"I know you do," Chloe said. "But I'm glad to work there. It's a very cool place, and Globe is super-cute."

Part of me had to wonder whether she'd remain so enamored of my adopted hometown after a few months of living here with hardly anything to do other than go to the movies or hike, and whether it would be quite so "cool" after she realized she couldn't just pop down the street to go to Ulta or the mall or wherever else it was that she liked to hang out.

Well, life was all about collecting new experiences. If, after the first six months, she decided she couldn't hack it here any longer, I'd completely understand. While I wouldn't have wanted to live anywhere else, I also understood that life in a small town wasn't exactly what all those Hallmark movies made it out to be.

"I'm glad you think so," I said. "And I'm glad you're okay with watching the shop on your own. Since you already have a set of keys, there probably isn't too much else you'll need, but you know I'm always a phone call away, just in case."

"And I'll have Victoria upstairs and Archie next door," she replied. "Everything is going to be fine, but I still like knowing your friends are so close by.

I'm sure they can help me with anything that might pop up."

If these had been normal circumstances, I would have thought the same thing. But with strange sigils appearing on my car and young men getting murdered for no apparent reason, I knew the current situation was anything but normal. Still, Archie would look out for Chloe because she was my younger sister, and Victoria would always be willing to help because that's just the kind of person she was. I might have been far more worried about my sister if it weren't for knowing my friends would be there to assist her if necessary.

"Oh, they absolutely will," I agreed. "But I'm pretty sure things should be fairly quiet, even with tomorrow being the last day of the big sale. Just don't let anyone push you into giving them a bigger discount than they're already getting."

"As if," Chloe responded, and I had to smile.

She might have left California, but I guessed my little sister would always be a Valley girl at heart.

Despite telling myself more than once that Chloe would be fine, I couldn't quite stop fretting about her being alone in the Airbnb tonight. Yes, it had been cleansed and she'd cast what felt like a very effective protection spell, but would it be enough?

"It's fine," Calvin told me during dinner, and I couldn't help startling a little.

"Was I being that obvious?"

"Sort of," he said, his mouth quirking at the corners. "But I understand. It's hard to go back into a place where something like that has happened."

"She was fine when we cleansed the house, though," I replied. "She's tougher than she looks. I suppose I'm just letting twenty years of not getting to be a big sister pile up on me all at once."

My husband looked thoughtful as he spooned some chicken cacciatore onto my plate. Even though it had been reheated from frozen, it was still damn good, and I was doing my best to savor every bite.

"I get it," he said. "And it makes me love you all that much more, watching you be protective of Chloe. But she's an adult, and she gets to make her own decisions."

Including going back to the Airbnb. I just wished I didn't feel so hinky about the situation.

Most likely, I was only responding that way because of the accident this afternoon and the discovery of the hex hidden under my license plate. True, I had no way of knowing whether Jack Speros's murderer and the person who'd scratched that sigil into the Jeep's paint were one and the same.

On the other hand, I had no reason to believe

that they weren't. All day long, my brain had been picking away at the problem, trying to see if it could turn up the smallest detail that might point to the person behind all this magical mayhem, but I couldn't think of a single suspect who controlled those sort of dark powers.

At least it didn't seem as though Chloe had been targeted at all, which meant she should be perfectly safe. No, she'd have a quiet night at the Airbnb, and then she'd head into work tomorrow morning, with the only truly frightening thing she needed to face being all the last-minute shoppers who would crowd into the place to take advantage of the final day of our big sale.

"It's true," I told my husband, and then cut off a piece of chicken and popped it in my mouth. Thank the Goddess that my appetite hadn't suffered much during my pregnancy, except for some queasy moments early on. True, the last couple of weeks I'd been getting full sooner than I would have liked and had cut back on my portions. Luckily, though, Dr. Carlisle said my weight gain was still right where she wanted it. "The last thing I want to do is hover."

"You're not hovering," Calvin said. "You're worrying, which is different but completely understandable."

I couldn't help smiling at those words. Some people might have said that Chloe wasn't my responsibility, and maybe she wasn't, at least in any legal sense of the word.

But she was family...and that made all the difference.

Despite all those reassurances, I didn't sleep well that night. Some of my restlessness could have been due to the simple fact that the baby decided to start practicing its field goal kicking at around eleven-thirty, but I thought it was more than that. Although I couldn't remember them clearly, my dreams had been disturbed as well, full of foreboding images that didn't make much sense once my eyes flared open and I stared up at the ceiling of the bedroom, only faintly illuminated by the glowing numerals on the alarm clock next to my bed.

Was I restless because my subconscious mind wouldn't leave me alone...or had the unknown user of magic pointed another hex at me, a slightly subtler one this time?

That thought wasn't reassuring at all.

Well, a glass of water would do me good. No way was I going to walk through the dark house into the kitchen, but I could head into the bathroom and get myself a drink there.

As soon as I sat up and pushed my legs over the

side of the bed, I heard Calvin's voice in the darkness.

"Everything okay?"

"I'm fine," I said, smiling a little as I thought of how many times I'd uttered those same two words today. "I just need some water."

He shifted against the pillows and said, "All right."

I pushed myself upright, still smiling. After all, my getting up in the middle of the night wasn't that strange an occurrence, not when it seemed as if sometimes I had to haul myself out of bed to use the bathroom every hour on the hour.

But I loved that he was being so vigilant, so attentive. I could tell he blamed himself for not going with me to my doctor's appointment this afternoon, even though I'd reassured him it was utterly routine and that he didn't need to miss any more work than he already had...and would in the near future.

Besides, having him behind the wheel wouldn't have prevented that crash. It was entirely possible he could have been hurt.

No, better that things had shaken out the way they did, even though I would be very glad if I never experienced another moment of terror like that again in my life.

The little nightlight in the bathroom provided just enough illumination for me to pour myself a glass of water. Our property had its own well, and the water was sweet and cold and fresh, easing the dryness in my mouth. I stood at the counter and drank the glass down, then wondered if I should pour myself another.

No, better not. I didn't want to be up and down even more times because I'd drunk too much water to slake my thirst.

I set the glass down. As I looked up, I caught a flash of movement in the darkness behind me.

Calvin, getting out of bed after all?

Something moved past my head, dark and icy cold.

Spectral fingers reached for me.

A terrified shriek left my lips, and I ran for the bed as fast as my distended belly would let me, somehow knowing if I could get there, I'd be safe.

"Calvin—" I gasped.

But he didn't move, only lay under the covers as still as a corpse.

No—

I reached for the sheets and blanket and pulled them back.

My husband's sightless eyes stared back at me, a red gash livid against his neck.

I screamed.

Chapter 13

BRUNCH BUNCH

A HAND SHOOK ME AWAKE. "SELENA! Selena!"

Air rattled in my throat as I pulled in a gasp and opened my eyes. Calvin was leaning over me, face urgent with worry.

Calvin. Oh, dear Goddess, he wasn't dead.

My arms went around him, and he pulled me close, holding me as I fought to pull more oxygen into my heaving lungs.

"Bad dream?" he asked, and I nodded, even as I continued to cling to him.

He was real. I had to keep reminding myself that he was real.

"The worst dream," I said. "Thank you for waking me up."

Strong, gentle fingers pushed at my disheveled bangs. "You kept making these little meeping noises, but then you tried to scream and were breathing like you'd just run a marathon, so I thought it was better to rouse you."

Thank the Goddess for that. I wasn't sure whether experiencing a terrifying dream was enough to cause a person to die of fright...and I never wanted to find out. Still holding on to him, I said, "Yes, it was much better that you woke me up."

"Do you want to talk about it?"

I looked at him, at his worried dark eyes, at the long black hair that was trying to escape the band he used to keep it confined while he slept. Although I knew now that it had only been a dream, some part of me worried I might give the horrible visions of the nightmare strength if I uttered them aloud.

So I shook my head and replied, "Not really. Let's go back to sleep."

No further dreams haunted my sleep that night, but when I woke up the next morning, I couldn't quite shake a troubling thought from my mind.

What if the same person who'd placed the hex on my car had also sent that nightmare to me?

I wanted to tell myself that was ridiculous, but I knew better. It was easier than some people might think to conjure a particularly bad dream and send it to roil the thoughts of an enemy.

But I wasn't anyone's enemy. I was just...Selena.

Pregnant women have awful dreams all the time, I thought. *It's all those hormones messing with your brain.*

Maybe that was true. Nevertheless, I was very, very glad that I'd be staying at home with Calvin today.

I did my best to shrug it off, and he seemed to guess that I wanted to put the nightmare well behind me, so he didn't ask. Instead, we watched TV together in the living room, unpacked the last few bibs and bobs for the nursery that had arrived this week but hadn't yet been set in their proper places, and even went and sat in the sun for a while after lunch, since it had turned out to be an unseasonably warm day and we wanted to enjoy it.

"Maybe we should plant some grass there," Calvin said, indicating the cactus-studded gravel wilderness that stretched beyond the patio. "Otherwise, there isn't much room to play in the yard."

No, there wasn't. And although I knew the baby wouldn't be toddling for a while yet, eventually we'd need to come up with some way to make our yard more kid-friendly. I'd always loved its wild beauty, but I also realized that it didn't offer many opportunities for a child to play safely.

"That's probably a good idea," I said. Yes, the property was xeriscaped to conserve water, but one patch of grass shouldn't be too much of a drain on the well. We could find a variety that was drought-tolerant and hardy, something that would provide a soft surface without requiring the kind of upkeep that grasses from other parts of the country would have needed in our hot climate. "Is there still enough time to plant?"

"I honestly don't know," Calvin replied. "I never worried about that kind of thing before now."

"Well, people are just setting out their spring plants," I said. "So we're probably safe. Maybe it's something you can look into on Saturday while I'm at brunch with the girls."

My husband nodded. "That could work. Maybe Tom will want to come along to the garden center. Does he know anything about growing lawns?"

The elegant Mediterranean-style house my mother and Tom shared in Woodland Hills definitely had beautiful grounds...but he also employed a gardener to make sure the grass was always a perfect, shimmering green. Maybe he'd mowed his own lawns back before his plumbing supply business really took off, although I had to believe those days were far enough behind him that he might not remember all that much.

Still, it would be kind of an outing for the guys. Tom had mentioned going up to Payson to golf, but Calvin had diplomatically shot down that idea, saying he didn't want to be that far away from me when I was so close to my due date.

Calvin hated golf, but he also didn't want to offend his father-in-law.

"I'm not sure," I said. "But I'll ask my mother if he's interested in giving you some advice."

My husband seemed fine with that idea, and a while later, we headed back inside. Although I'd been doing my best to avoid my phone and allow Chloe to handle her first day at the store on her own, my willpower failed then, and I picked it up when I went into my office so I could give her a quick call.

"Once in a Blue Moon, how can I help you?"

It was exactly the same way I always answered the phone when I was at work, and I couldn't help smiling—even as I lowered myself onto the couch and heard it creak slightly under my weight.

Maybe it would be a good thing if this baby came early. Beached whales had nothing on me.

"Hi, Chloe, it's Selena," I said. "I just thought I'd check to see how things were going."

"Oh, fine," she replied. "It's been kind of steady all day but nothing too crazy."

"And there hasn't been anything...strange?"

Her voice sharpened slightly. "Should there be?"

I hadn't told her about the hex because I hadn't wanted her to worry any more than she already was. "No, no," I said hurriedly. "I suppose I'm just a little on edge. I've tried using the Tarot to help me figure out who killed Jack, but I didn't get anything definitive."

"Same here," Chloe said. "Usually, I'll get a pull that provides some illumination, but nothing seems to make much sense to me. No dreams, either."

I supposed I should have guessed that my little sister would also have turned to the cards for some insight into the identity and motivations of the murderer. While she didn't have as many years of experience as I did, that didn't mean she wasn't capable of using that particular method of divination. As to why she hadn't experienced any true dreams during this episode, I couldn't say for sure. I honestly didn't know how often she had them, and frankly, after the nightmare I'd suffered the evening before, I wasn't about to wish vivid dreams on anyone.

"Well, if it's supposed to come, it will," I told her. "The universe has its own timing, and we can't force it."

"Maybe," Chloe responded, although now she sounded almost dubious. "Right now I'm just waiting to hear from Alec. He said he was going to make his case to the judge at two o'clock today."

That was only about forty minutes from now. I was surprised she'd been able to concentrate at all, with such a momentous decision hanging over her, but maybe it had helped to be at the store focusing on customers rather than brooding over what the judge might or might not say to determine her fate.

"I'm sure it will all work out fine," I said. "And I won't keep you. But call me as soon as you hear something, okay?"

"I will," she promised. "Or at least, I'll call you after I call my parents. Talk to you soon!"

We ended the call there, and I set my phone back down on the bookcase where it had been sitting. As I did so, my gaze moved to the shelf that held all my Tarot cards.

Should I try again?

Or maybe it was time to deploy my pendulum, although working with it could sometimes be tricky.

I stood there for a moment, hands on my hips —which definitely felt a good bit wider than they had six months ago—and held myself still, letting the calm, lightly incense-scented air surround me and bring me to a place where I could make the right decision. Off to one side, a clock ticked, its rhythmic sound almost hypnotic.

All right, the pendulum it was.

Both my favorite fluorite pendulum and the pretty mat with butterflies and twining leaves that I used for divination in the springtime sat on a separate bookshelf, so I gathered them up and took them over to the altar. After I set them down, I got out a lighter and touched its flame to the incense cone that sat waiting in a celadon bowl. At once, the faint scent that always seemed to drift on the air in that room grew stronger as smoke began to swirl upward.

Once again, I let myself stand there quietly, allowing my thoughts to begin to slow so they could formulate the correct questions to ask. Working with a pendulum meant framing everything in questions that could be answered with a simple yes or no; while there were pendulum mats out there printed with all the letters of the alphabet and sometimes numbers one through ten, I'd never had much luck working with them to get more precise responses.

No, it was much easier to keep things to a set of simple binary equations.

Which meant I couldn't ask who had killed Jack Speros. Instead, I had to come up with a way to make the questions I asked point back to either yes or no.

Did Jack Speros know his killer?

The fluorite pendulum had been dangling

motionless over the mat, but now it swung hard over to *Yes.*

Not much doubt in that answer. I hated to ask the follow-up, but I would have been remiss if I didn't.

Did Chloe Fairfield kill Jack Speros?

The pendulum sailed back and forth just as hard this time, except it went in the other direction, right over to *No.*

That it was so emphatic in its reply made me feel a lot better. No, I really hadn't thought Chloe could be the murderer—not just because I'd seen her aura and knew hers wasn't the soul of a killer, but also because the simple physics of the case indicated that someone barely five foot five and who maybe weighed a hundred and ten pounds on a good day certainly wasn't capable of throttling a healthy young man with six inches and at least sixty or seventy pounds on her.

Still, even though I was very, very glad that my sister hadn't been involved in Jack's death, the mystery had only deepened.

He'd known his killer...which meant it couldn't have been anyone local. Not that I'd truly suspected such a thing, since he knew no one here except Chloe and there wouldn't have been any reason for the murder, except possibly a break-in and a burglary gone wrong.

That theory didn't make any sense, though, because there hadn't been any sign of forced entry.

I ran a hand through my hair, feeling the silky strands fall back on my shoulders, heavy and straight. Once or twice I'd thought about cutting it shorter, since I'd heard horror stories about long hair and grabby baby hands, but I just couldn't bring myself to do that.

No, I'd just resign myself to ponytails and messy updos for the first couple of years.

All right, so a stranger had come to Globe for the sole purpose of killing Jack Speros. But why? According to Chloe, he wasn't a person who had any real enemies...except possibly Bryce Arsenault... and no one should have had any motive to get rid of him.

And if her accounts of how he'd been desperate to get her back after she broke up with him were correct, it wasn't as if we were dealing with some kind of love triangle here. There hadn't been a desperate third party who'd decided to drive to Globe and pull some kind of *Fatal Instinct* maneuver. Then again, people kept all sorts of secrets from one another. Even if the suspect wasn't some woman who'd had her own designs on Jack, that didn't mean there might not be someone in his past...like Bryce Arsenault...who had a vendetta against him, for whatever reason.

The problem was, I didn't know even where to

begin to look for such a person. Chloe had offered me one possible suspect, but she obviously hadn't been able to think of anyone except Bryce who'd had any kind of negative interactions with her ex-boyfriend.

Both my feet and my head were starting to hurt. Although I wanted to solve this mystery, I also wanted to make sure my child had an easy, drama-free entrance into the world.

Which meant it was time to sit down on the couch for a while.

I headed into the living room, where Calvin was sitting in one of the armchairs, reading. Always nonfiction, though, this time a book about the Pueblo revolt in New Mexico.

He set it aside as I entered and gave me an expectant look. "Everything okay?"

"It's fine," I said. "Chloe said Alec is going in front of the judge shortly to try to get the case dismissed. And I tried working with my pendulum, but all it would tell me is that the killer is someone Jack Speros knew and that it definitely wasn't my sister."

"Well, that's something, I suppose," Calvin replied. "At least that means it wasn't anyone here in Globe."

A conclusion I'd already drawn, which meant I didn't have a whole lot to go on right now.

"It's too bad his parents are so hostile toward

Chloe and her family," I said next. "Otherwise, I might try to talk to them and see if they could provide any clues. Unfortunately, I have a feeling if I tried to reach out, they'd just shoot me down."

"Probably," Calvin agreed. "They seemed pretty set on wanting to pin the blame on your sister, even though it's obvious she didn't have anything to do with their son's death."

"And I've already talked to Chloe, and she doesn't seem to know anything." I paused there, knowing I was starting to sound a little whiny. Not that anyone could blame me, given the circumstances, but since there wasn't much point in going over the same ground for the tenth time and expecting something different, I decided to leave it alone. "I suppose we just need to wait and see what the judge says. If he makes this whole thing go away, then it's sort of a moot point, I guess."

Calvin inclined his head ever so slightly. Not a large gesture, but we'd been together long enough that I knew what he was thinking. Even if the judge dismissed Chloe's case, I'd have a hard time letting all this go...especially since in my heart of hearts I knew that the hex on my Jeep and Jack's murder were related, even if I hadn't been able to put the pieces together yet.

And while I thought there might be a number of people out there who had a bone to pick with me for sending their relatives to prison, I couldn't see how they could be involved in any of this, not with all the dark magic that seemed to be flying around town.

Then again, I supposed a practitioner of that sort of magic might want to keep it on the down-low.

Calvin's phone rang then, and he fished it out of his pocket. "Calvin here," he said, then paused, as though allowing the caller to go into detail as to their reason for reaching out. He murmured, "Mm-hmm," a couple of times, which didn't help at all to illuminate what the person was saying on the other end of the call. Once they were done, though, he said, "Thanks," then ended the call and returned the phone to his pocket.

I sent him an expectant look, although I managed to refrain from asking, *Well?*

"That was Ben," he told me, the amused light in his eyes letting me know he'd seen right away how hard it had been for me to prevent myself from asking who the caller had been. "He was able to find Bryce Arsenault. He never came back to California, but is still living in Vermont, where he's finishing up his final year of college. He also works in the school's library."

That all sounded pretty respectable to me, so I wasn't sure I could buy into the idea that Bryce had followed Jack to Globe to carry out his blood-thirsty revenge for what had happened at Cal State

Northridge almost four years earlier. Then again, if I'd learned anything since I moved to Arizona and started solving mysteries, it was that people weren't always who they appeared to be on the surface.

Did Bryce's evil side include scratching evil sigils on my car?

I wasn't at all sure about that.

"And he's been in Vermont this whole time?" I pressed. "No unexpected trips to visit family in California?"

"Ben didn't say," Calvin replied. "But I'm sure if there had been any evidence of recent trips like that, he would have mentioned it."

Most likely. I didn't know Ben Ironhorse well, but he seemed like a thorough kind of guy, not the sort of person who would leave loose ends dangling.

"Then I suppose that's that," I said, trying not to sound too defeated. After all, while it felt to me as though Bryce Arsenault was a dead end, I still couldn't say for sure that I was ready to write him off as a suspect.

"I suppose so," my husband replied, and seemed content to leave it there. Or at least, he could tell my brain was still churning away at the problem, trying to poke it from all sides to see what it might eventually reveal. I supposed I should be relieved that he would never tell me what to do...

unless he thought my actions might endanger the child I was carrying.

And that absolutely wasn't going to happen. The accident had been close.

Too close.

I knew I wouldn't be able to focus on reading, so I turned on the TV and watched one of my home decorating shows on Discovery+. However, I kept the sound low enough that it wouldn't disturb Calvin, who'd picked his book up again when he realized I wasn't in the mood for further conversation.

And when my cell phone rang, I immediately took the remote and paused the show I was watching, then grabbed the phone and put it to my ear.

"Hey, Selena," Chloe said, sounding breathless. "The judge dismissed the case!"

I blinked. Even though this was the outcome we'd all been hoping for, I still couldn't help being a little shocked that it had happened so quickly. "That's great news!" I replied.

"It is," she said, although something in her tone didn't sound quite as happy as I'd thought it would be.

Maybe I shouldn't probe...but leaving things alone really wasn't in my nature.

"Did the judge put any stipulations on the dismissal?"

"No," Chloe said quickly. "He said there wasn't enough solid evidence to merit continuing with the case against me, and he threw out the whole thing. It's just...."

The words trailed off, and I heard a distinct sigh come through the phone's tiny speaker.

"Just what?" I asked.

"It's just that...." Her words faded again, but then she continued, her voice sounding a bit stronger. "It's just that this way, people won't know for sure that I'm innocent. I could tell that some of the customers who came to the store this morning thought the whole thing was kind of shady, since they kept giving me the side-eye when they thought I wasn't looking."

"You said it was quiet at the store this morning," I responded, my tone growing a little sharper.

She sighed again. "It was. And I mean, it wasn't as if anyone came right up to me and called me a murderer to my face or anything. But I still got the vibe, you know? And since I'd really like to stay here, it's going to be hard if there are a bunch of people in town who think I got away with murder."

"They're not going to think that," I said at once. "Judge Adler doesn't pull any punches. If he thought the case merited going to trial, he would have said so. People will understand. And they'll also know that I wouldn't have you working at the store if I didn't trust you."

Even as I spoke, however, I had to wonder how accurate my words truly were. After all, I'd kind of blown it with Melanie Knowles. Yes, I'd figured out her villainy in the end...but only at the last minute. There definitely could be a subset of Globe's population who might still think my judgment was a wee bit faulty.

Well, I'd worry about that later. The important thing was that Chloe wouldn't be going to trial, and that took a lot of pressure off all of us.

"You think so?" she asked, the plaintive note in her voice telling me she wanted reassurance more than truth right then.

"Yes," I said firmly. "I do."

Even though they were relieved that Chloe had been exonerated, the Fairfields decided to extend their stay in Globe a few more days. Whether that was because they expected their daughter to change her mind about living here or whether they wanted to be absolutely sure everything was settled with her before they headed back to Southern California, I didn't know for sure.

"But they're not pressuring me or anything,"

Chloe said as we drove over to my mother and Tom's place for our girls' brunch. She'd insisted on being my chauffeur, even though it was at least ten minutes out of her way to pick me up at the house.

I hadn't argued too much, though, since I was supposed to stay away from behind the wheel and I could tell she was eager to help. Calvin would have driven me, of course, but this just made more sense, especially since he'd already set out to meet Tom at the local nursery.

And I had to admit it felt good to put the murder investigation and my worries about the hex on my car aside for a while, and to simply be with good friends. My mother had outdone herself with the flowers and the table settings...although I had a feeling Victoria had offered some helpful advice along the way.

Everyone was there—Josie and Hazel and Victoria, and Terry Woodrow and Sofia Barnes and Joyce Lewis and Chloe herself. Once again, I wondered whether I should have invited Heather to brunch, even though I understood that we barely knew each other and it might have been strange to attend a brunch thrown by the woman who'd had a child with her husband so many years before.

Doubt was cast aside as everyone congratulated Chloe on having the charges dismissed. She flushed and then looked over at me, saying, "It was very good news. But this brunch is supposed to be about Selena, right?"

"It's about getting together with friends and family," I replied. "I'm not interested in being the center of attention."

Victoria smiled. "You're sure about that?"

"Positive."

Her blue eyes twinkled. "Then I guess this is a good time to share the news. Archie and I are having a baby, too."

Of course the table had to erupt in congratulations, with everyone asking her when the baby was due.

"Early October," she said. "Just a week or so after Hazel."

"It sounds like we've got a real baby boom going on here in Globe," Hazel added, and Josie beamed.

"And that's a wonderful thing. It will be so amazing to have all my good friends expanding our little family here that much more."

It would. I looked around the table at all the smiling faces there and thought that Chloe had made a good choice. No, we didn't have L.A.'s glitz and glamour, but we had a real community, one that was much more welcoming than I might have thought at first, considering the way Henry Lewis and I had butted heads from almost the very beginning. He'd come to accept me, though...well, mostly. And Sofia was doing very well, even though she'd only been here a few months. No romance in her life yet, but I supposed that was okay. It was going to take a while to undo the damage inflicted by her controlling, murderous ex-partner, and for now, she was just focused on making her charming brewpub one of our little town's premier destinations.

We were all exactly where we were supposed to be.

But that didn't mean I didn't intend to find out who really killed Jack Speros...even if I had to continue the investigation from a hospital bed.

Chapter 14

PUT IT ON REPEAT

CHLOE DROVE ME HOME AFTER BRUNCH, A little past one o'clock. She couldn't linger because she wanted to get back to Once in a Blue Moon and not miss out completely on all that Saturday afternoon prime shopping time.

"Will Calvin be back soon?" she asked, looking a little anxious as she seemed to notice that my husband's big white Durango was still missing from the driveway.

"He texted me as he was leaving the garden center," I replied. It was sweet of her to be worried about leaving me here alone, but I knew it wasn't an issue. "He should be here in ten minutes or so. It's fine."

That piece of information made her expression brighten. "Oh, okay. Then I guess it's all right."

I assured her that it was, then pushed myself

out of her VW and waddled over to the front door while she turned the car around and headed down the long gravel drive that led to our private lane. With any luck, she would be back out on the main road before Calvin got here; two cars could pass on the narrow street that led to our property, but it was something of a squeeze.

When I went inside, I paused for a moment to pet Sadie, who of course had come bounding up the second I entered the house, then glanced around. Nothing felt out of place, and yet something inside made me glad Calvin would be home soon.

It was silly to feel that way, though—I'd made sure the house was thoroughly protected, and there was no sign that anyone had been here in my absence.

Just the heebie-jeebies, I told myself. *The accident and that horrible dream the other night have put you off balance.*

Probably. I especially didn't want to feel this way after spending such a lovely couple of hours with my friends and my mother. Just because I'd suffered a couple of shocks lately didn't mean that anything was wrong.

My Jeep was still in limbo, since the mechanic hadn't yet been able to find anything physically wrong with it and the insurance adjuster wouldn't even make it out to Globe to look over the vehicle until Monday. Under normal circumstances, I would have gone to Gilbert or Mesa to rent a car so I wouldn't be without wheels, but these weren't exactly normal circumstances.

I headed into the kitchen, figuring a glass of water would help dispel some of my current hinkiness. And that was where Calvin found me a few minutes later, sipping some water as I leaned against the counter, even as I told myself I should have gone into the living room to sit down.

"How was brunch?" he asked.

"It was great," I said. There didn't seem to be any point in telling him about my recent bout of nerves, not when there wasn't any physical reason for me to have reacted that way when I came into the house. No, I was just letting my imagination run away with itself again. "And guess what? Victoria's expecting, too!"

At once, Calvin came over and hugged me. "That's great news," he said, then paused. "Or at least, I suppose it is. I can't really imagine Archie changing a diaper, can you?"

I chuckled, all my worries of a moment earlier evaporating in the face of such a comic mental scene. "Not really," I replied. "But I suppose he'll get the hang of it eventually."

The corners of my husband's dark eyes crinkled in amusement. "Hopefully. Did you have any idea they were even planning to start a family?"

"None," I said, reflecting that Victoria had been holding her cards pretty close to the vest on this one. "I always got the impression she wanted to take some time to focus on really getting the design studio up and running before they even talked about having kids...but sometimes this stuff just happens."

"That it does," Calvin remarked. Our baby was very much planned, even if we hadn't known exactly how the timing was going to work out, but I got the feeling he was thinking of his own large family and how his four brothers and sisters had so many kids of their own. Those children were definitely wanted, even if some of them had been surprises at the time.

The conversation moved on to what fun it was going to be for all of us to have babies around the same age, even if Calvin's and mine was making an earlier appearance in the world than Hazel's or Victoria's. Right then, I wished I wasn't feeling so confined to the house, because if I'd been at the store, I would have been able to go over and congratulate Archie in person on the impending arrival. Yes, I'd already given Victoria my best wishes, but it wasn't quite the same thing.

But my little world was changing, and I'd just have to roll with it.

Later that afternoon, I got a text from Chloe.

My parents want to go out 2nite to celebrate the dismissal. Can U & Cal make it to the Gold Dust @ 7?

Part of me wanted to decline. I'd already gone to brunch at my mother's house, and that seemed like enough social gatherings for one day.

On the other hand, the gesture felt like an obvious olive branch from the Fairfields, and it seemed rude to decline. Also, since the restaurant at the Gold Dust casino was on tribal lands, it was only about a five-minute drive from our house and therefore felt a lot more approachable than going back into Globe.

I asked Calvin if he was okay with the plan, and he said, "If you are. It feels like kind of a lot for one day."

Echoing what I'd thought just a moment before. However, I only shrugged and said, "Yes, but it's close, and it's not as if we'll be out late. I think we should."

"Then it's fine with me."

Which was pretty much exactly what I'd thought he would say, but still, I was glad he was on board with the plan.

So I texted Chloe back and told her that was fine and that we were looking forward to it. Afterward, though, I found myself restless and once again headed into my office, even though I knew I would have been better served to spend the time between now and our dinner date with the Fairfields sitting in the living room with my feet up.

I was getting awfully tired of that, though. I wasn't an invalid, just a pregnant woman who was ready to pop any day now.

My gaze roamed over the decks of Tarot cards on my bookshelf. Most of the time I used my trusty Everyday Witch deck, but I still hoarded way more decks than I probably should, occasionally reaching out to a different set of cards when my Everyday Witch ones didn't seem up to the task, for whatever reason.

Maybe now was the time to try something different. Yes, Chloe wouldn't be going to trial, but I still had no idea who had followed Jack Speros to her Airbnb and throttled him in the living room there.

I went over to the bookshelf and let my fingers trail across the various decks there, looking for that inner twinge or tingle to let me know which one would be better suited for my current purposes.

And then it settled on the Light Seers tarot.

Well, that seemed appropriate. I was definitely trying to shine a light on the situation and find my way to the truth.

I pulled out the deck and took it over to my altar. Because it had been so long since I'd used these particular cards, I lit some palo santo incense and used the purifying smoke to cleanse the deck and ready it for the reading.

Just inhaling the clean, aromatic smoke drifting up from the cone made me feel a little better. While it had been wonderful to see everyone, being around that many people at once could also be draining, and giving myself this time to be in my sacred space and alone with my books and cards and crystals was restorative in a way I wasn't sure I could ever fully explain.

But now that I'd cleansed the deck and made myself as open to the universe's suggestions as I possibly could, it was time to see what this particular set of cards had to tell me.

I shuffled and shuffled, waiting for the small inner sign that would let me know it was time to stop and pull a card. It took a long time, and I began to wonder whether I should have switched decks. Every once in a while, I couldn't get the Tarot to vibe with me no matter what I did.

At last, though, my fingertips tingled, and I stopped so I could pull the first card out of the deck.

The Devil. In this particular deck, he wore the face of a handsome man with wild black hair, one hand reached forward in a beckoning gesture, but still.

Not this again, I thought. It wouldn't be the first time when I'd had a second card pull turn out to be a mirror image of one I'd already done, but I'd really been hoping for some fresh insights this time around.

The second card was the Seven of Swords.

I wanted to let out a bitter chuckle. However, even though I'd told Calvin I was going to my office to work with my cards, I had a feeling a single unexpected sound would bring him over here to check on me.

With a feeling of inevitability, I reached for the third card, fully expecting to see the Emperor again. However, the card looking up at me was the Queen of Cups, reversed.

Generally, she was a positive card. When reversed, however, she could mean co-dependency, unhealthy relationships.

Not so surprising when juxtaposed with the Devil and the Seven of Swords. But why had she appeared now, rather than the Emperor?

I didn't know. While I'd been hoping for some additional illumination, all I'd really gotten was a deepening of the mystery.

My gaze moved to the crystal ball on its lower shelf. Grandma Ellen knew about my pregnancy and was happy for me, but I hadn't contacted her lately, knowing she could see what was going on in my life when she needed to and that in general, it was better not to reach out too often to interrupt her in her existence in the afterlife.

But I was feeling awfully stuck here. And Chloe, although not related to Grandma Ellen by blood, was still my little sister. Wouldn't she care that someone so closely connected to me would continue to have this cloud hanging over her unless I could somehow find my way to the truth?

Well, that seemed to settle things.

It wasn't much fun to bend over and fetch the heavy crystal ball and its wooden stand from the bookshelf, but somehow I managed it. However, I had a feeling I'd have to ask Calvin to put it back for me once I was done.

I placed my hands on the crystal's surface, feeling it warm slightly with the contact. Keeping my voice to a murmur, I said, "Grandma Ellen, I need to talk to you."

The interior of the crystal ball remained clear, which was never a good sign. When she appeared, a swirling mist usually filled the ball first, and then she followed a little later...sometimes a lot later. Now, though, I couldn't see any sign of her.

That didn't mean I intended to give up.

"Grandma Ellen, it's important."

At last, a fine mist began to appear inside the ball. I held my breath, as though fearing that the slightest puff of air against the crystal might make the mist disappear and my grandmother might never show up at all.

But more mist swirled, and then a moment

later, I could see my grandmother's face staring back at me. As always, she appeared as she had when she passed away, younger than the forty-two she'd been, with blonde hair waving over her shoulders and the same deep blue eyes my mother and I shared as well.

She didn't look too surprised, which told me she had at least a passing idea of what had been happening in Globe over the past week.

"Selena, you really need to be tending to your own house," she said without preamble, and I blinked at her.

"Do you know something I don't?" I demanded, and she gave me one of her Mona Lisa smiles, telling me that while she might possess knowledge I didn't, she wasn't inclined to share it with me.

"What's there to know?" she responded. "You're due to give birth in less than two weeks. Running around trying to solve a murder might not be the best use of your energy right now, especially since it seems as if your younger sister isn't in any danger of going to prison."

Wow, Grandma Ellen really had been keeping pretty close tabs. Then again, I supposed that wasn't too strange. I had to believe she'd been watching my doings much more carefully than she might normally would have, since her first great-grandchild was due to make an appearance almost any day now.

"No," I said, "but still, she wants to live here in Globe, and she doesn't want to start off with a bunch of people thinking she's a murderer. It just makes sense that I would want to track down the person responsible—and not just for her sake. No one wants a killer walking around loose, you know?"

Grandma Ellen's lips—wearing their usual coating of Revlon's Cherries in the Snow lipstick—curved in a faint smile. "No, they don't," she said. "And I have to say I'm glad you were finally able to meet your sister. I wasn't around to offer my opinion, but I never liked the way your mother and Jordan made sure to keep you entirely out of his other children's lives. The two of them weren't together, of course, and yet I didn't believe that meant you should never get to know your siblings."

Well, at least Grandma Ellen was on my side when it came to that particular topic. I hadn't pushed my mother on the subject, partly because the age gap meant I would probably never have a whole lot in common with my half-siblings, and partly because by the time I really started to think it was wrong that I had a family I never got to meet, I was old enough to have a whole host of other things to distract me.

"Chloe is a great girl," I said. "She doesn't deserve what's happened to her."

"But she has you providing all kinds of support," my grandmother countered. "And while I agree it would be wonderful if you could clear her name, I don't think it's going to damage her life irreparably if you can't."

I planted my hands on my hips. "Which is your way of telling me you're not going to help me with this."

Once again, she gave me a half smile. "At the risk of repeating my words from previous murder cases you've investigated, you have all the clues you need. It's how you put them together that's important. Just remember that Jack Speros knew his murderer. It wasn't someone from Globe."

After uttering those words, she faded away, and the mists that had been swirling around her face disappeared as well. I would have tried to call her back, but I knew when she departed like that, she had no intention of returning any time soon.

It wasn't someone from Globe.

A notion I'd been entertaining for a while, but my grandmother's words had seemed pretty emphatic.

Could it be that Bryce Arsenault really was the killer? He certainly wasn't from Globe, and he definitely had a reason to be angry with Jack Speros. I just couldn't say for sure that Bryce's anger rose to the level of cold-blooded murder, especially since there wasn't any clear evidence that he'd left Vermont any time in the recent past. Ben Ironhorse should have located records of any flights Bryce had taken, and it wasn't as though you could just jump in a car and drive from Burlington to our little corner of southeast Arizona in the blink of an eye. No, that sort of trip would require some planning, and as far as I could tell, there was no indication that he'd ever been anywhere except where he was supposed to be. Then again, if he'd paid cash for his gas and his motel rooms and had driven fast, he could have hidden the expedition from any online searches and still gotten here in a couple of days. I couldn't discount his involvement, even if it seemed like a long shot to me.

Which made me feel as though I was farther from an answer to the mystery than when I'd started.

As best I could, I put my worries behind me as I changed into the pretty green dress that was the one nice piece I owned that still fit and managed to be halfway flattering. Calvin had noticed that I'd used my crystal ball—obviously, since I had to ask him to put it back for me—but he seemed to sense that I didn't want to talk about what I'd seen, since he was quiet as he helped me into the Durango and we backed out of the garage.

Once we were on the road, though, he said, "This is supposed to be a celebration, you know."

"I know," I replied, and managed a wan smile. "And I promise I'll be cheerful once we get to the restaurant. I just wish I had some good news to give Chloe."

"She already got her good news for the day," my husband said. "She doesn't have to stand trial or worry about going to jail. I know you wanted to have Jack's murderer wrapped up in a bow, but sometimes life doesn't work that way."

No, it didn't. I did my best to remind myself that everyone had thought the murderer from Josie's brewing competition was safely behind bars before the contest was even over, but I'd still believed the real killer was out there somewhere... and I hadn't given up. I'd managed to ferret out the perpetrator—Sofia's ex-boyfriend and ex-partner—although the competition was done by then.

There was no reason to believe I couldn't pull off the same ninth-inning rebound here, to use a sports phrase. Then again, I'd had a lot more clues to go on last time.

Which didn't necessarily mean anything.

We pulled into the parking lot of the Gold Dust, which was fairly crowded that Saturday night. I was kind of surprised the Fairfields had been able to get a reservation for five at such late notice, since the casino's restaurant was the only place close by where you could have something resembling a fine dining experience and most people in town went there for their birthday and anniversary celebrations.

Well, maybe Chloe's parents had just gotten lucky. Maybe there had been a cancellation or something.

Calvin helped me out of the Durango, and the two of us made our way over to the entrance. The Fairfields were already seated in the waiting area, although Jordan stood up as Calvin and I approached.

"Thank you for coming on such short notice," he said. "We wanted to do something to show our appreciation for everything you've done."

"Oh, it wasn't that much," I replied. Maybe it would have been better to accept my bio father's praise without any kind of demurral, but I couldn't help feeling I'd still been kind of a failure, considering I hadn't been able to figure out who'd killed Jack Speros.

"But it was," he said. His tone was firm, telling me he wasn't going to accept any kind of self-deprecating talk when it came to my efforts to clear Chloe's name. In his mind, I'd succeeded, since the charges had been dismissed and she no longer had to worry about legal retaliation connected to Jack's death.

Luckily, the hostess called the Fairfields' name right then, and we had to break off the conversation so she could lead us to our table. Calvin helped me into my seat, and everyone else sat down as well.

A few minutes passed as we all looked over the menu and decided on what we wanted—I almost always went for filet mignon and tonight was no different—but after we'd placed our orders, Heather folded her hands on the table and gave me a grateful look.

"What Jordan told you is how all of us are feeling," she said. "I can't tell you what a relief it is to know that Chloe has been cleared of all connection to Jack's murder. It was a terrible thing, and we feel awful for the Speros family, but at least we can all start to move on."

I managed a smile, even as Chloe sent the very smallest of sideways glances in my direction. That was about all we could allow ourselves, though, since it was obvious her parents were ready to put this mess behind them.

"That was always my hope for everyone," I responded. "And I really am grateful to Chloe for staying here and helping with the shop."

Judging by the way neither Jordan nor Heather said anything right away, I could tell they still weren't all that thrilled about her decision to make a new life here in Globe. However, it also seemed they were trying to make their peace with the situation...and that they definitely didn't want to get into an argument at a dinner that was supposed to be a celebration.

"It's taken a load off both Selena's and my minds," Calvin put in. Trust my husband to do his best to be the peacemaker—his Libra nature asserting itself, I supposed.

But his words had done what he'd intended them to do—namely, reminding Chloe's parents of how much their daughter was doing to help us during what was already a busy and stressful time.

Jordan nodded, and the corners of Heather's mouth lifted slightly. Right then, the waitress came back with our drink orders, which in my case was plain water. I'd drunk sparkling water for a while to make the plain beverage feel a little more festive, but lately, the carbonation had been too much for my stomach to handle.

The Fairfields had cocktails, since obviously they hadn't taken the same vow to abstain during my pregnancy that Calvin had. Chloe, although old enough to drink, had only asked for iced tea, although I didn't know whether that was because she simply wasn't in the mood or whether she was skipping it tonight out of deference to my condition.

"I like working at the shop," she declared, clearly wanting to add her voice to the conversation. "It's so peaceful, even when it's full of customers. Good vibes, you know?"

I did know, just because I'd been very careful about the items I placed for sale in the store, making sure they all were able to contribute to the harmony of the place.

"Still, your housing situation isn't exactly stable," Heather said.

While I could understand her worry, I knew I needed to do what I could to reassure her that Chloe wouldn't be homeless once her run at Hazel's Airbnb was over. "My friend Josie has a friend who has lots of Airbnbs," I replied. "I'm sure Chloe can move to one of Mavis's homes when Hazel's guests come to town later this month. And obviously, the whole time we'll be looking for a permanent place for her."

Although I didn't say it out loud, I had to hope Heather would understand that I meant I would be there to support Chloe every step of the way, up to and including taking care of whatever security deposits she might need once we did find a forever place for her to stay.

The message must have gotten through, because Heather relaxed against the back of her seat and reached for her martini. "Well, that's good to hear."

To my relief, the conversation moved on to other topics after that, up to and including the all-important subject of the new baby's name. Calvin and I had our favorites, of course, but because we didn't know the sex of our child, we had to be content with a top three for either gender and hope that inspiration would strike once the baby had made its entrance into the world and we gazed down into his or her face.

Jordan might have gotten the slightest wistful look when I mentioned how my mother had named me Selena because she'd thought I would be born under the sign of Cancer, and I wondered if he ever regretted not being there when I came into the world.

Maybe. But every indication showed he was happy with the way his life had turned out...and so was I.

As dinner was winding down, I excused myself to go to the ladies' room. At once, Chloe plucked the napkin out of her lap and said, "Oh, I need to go, too."

We headed off there together...even as I had the sneaking suspicion that this wasn't merely about having to use the restroom.

To my relief—in more ways than one—she waited until we'd both taken care of business and were washing our hands.

"I didn't want to say anything in front of my

parents," she began. "And I know it's a huge imposition, but I was wondering if I could come back and stay with you and Calvin for a couple of days. Just until I can find another place to crash," she went on hastily, as I had a feeling I hadn't been quite able to hide the surprise on my face.

"Is something wrong at Hazel's Airbnb?" I asked. "Have you felt something?"

Immediately, Chloe shook her head. "No, nothing like that," she replied. "It's not like Jack's ghost suddenly decided to appear or something. But it still feels weird to be there. I just think I'd sleep better at your house. I'll totally get it if you need to say no, though."

Worry was clear in every inch of her pretty, pixieish features, so I knew I needed to soothe those fears as best I could. "It's fine," I said. "The baby isn't due for another week and a half, so we can put you up until then. Or even after," I added with a grin. "I'm sure both Calvin and I would be fine with having an extra pair of hands around for diaper duty."

Her nose wrinkled, although she corrected herself almost at once. "I can do that," she said stoutly, and my smile only broadened.

"It's fine," I said. "I don't expect you to handle dirty diapers...just like I really don't expect you to hang around to put up with 3 a.m. feedings and the rest of it. We'll get something figured out."

"You're sure?" she asked, dark gray eyes shining with relief.

"Absolutely. Just go back to the Airbnb and get your stuff, and then head out to the house. Your parents won't even have to know."

"Thanks, Selena."

I assured her it was fine, and the two of us headed back out to the table where the rest of our party was waiting. Calvin and I thanked the Fairfields for dinner—it was their treat—and then everyone walked over to their respective vehicles, with Chloe and her parents pointing their cars toward town while my husband and I got in his Durango and went in the opposite direction.

"Chloe's coming to stay with us for a few more days," I said once we were out of the parking lot, and he lifted a surprised eyebrow.

"Really? Is everything okay?"

"As far as I can tell," I replied. "I just think she's feeling hinky, and I get it. I'm sure we'll be able to get her into one of Mavis's Airbnbs in the next day or so."

Preferably not the one where Dillon James had been killed by his murderous agent. Although I knew the place wasn't haunted, I still thought it was probably better to keep Chloe away from any crime scenes.

"If you're sure," my husband said, with a pointed glance at my swollen belly.

The baby had been mostly quiescent during dinner, but it chose that time to kick. I blinked, thinking, *Soon, little one.*

"Oh, I'm sure," I said. I didn't know why, but something inside me was telling me this was the right thing to do.

We needed to keep our family together.

About a half hour after Calvin and I got back from our dinner with the Fairfields, Chloe showed up carrying two overnight bags and wearing an expression that was half relief and half worry.

"You're really, really sure this is okay?" she said as I led her to the guest bedroom so she could drop off her bags.

"It's fine," I said. "And Calvin's fine with it, too. Tomorrow I'll call Mavis and see which one of her places is available. Sometimes they're all booked up, but since we haven't hit spring break yet, I'm hoping at least one will be empty."

Chloe set both the bags down on the guest room bed. Since the room was fairly large, we had a queen in there, along with a set of nightstands and a dresser and a mirror. I hadn't gotten around to adding many personal touches, mostly because Calvin and I had gone back and forth on whether to keep the space as a guest room or turn it into a play area for the baby, but at least it was functional and had a bathroom just down the hall.

"That sounds good," my sister said. "And I'll stay out of your hair tonight. I'm kind of sleepy and just want to crash early."

A plan I could definitely get on board with. Maybe Chloe's definition of "early" was scrolling through her phone for a couple of hours before she finally decided to go to sleep, but every inch of my body was telling me it had been a long day and that I needed to be in bed sooner rather than later.

"You have a good night," I told her, then headed out to the living room, where Calvin had sat down in one of the armchairs and was petting Sadie. He hadn't turned on the TV, though, telling me he also thought it was a good idea to go to sleep almost immediately.

"Ready to get to bed?" he said, and I nodded. Once upon a time, that question would have probably led to the sort of activities that had resulted in the child I was carrying, but right now, I was only thinking of sweet, sweet slumber.

"Thought you'd never ask," I replied.

No one seemed too inclined to get up early the next morning, even though we'd all been pretty much asleep before ten o'clock. Instead, Calvin and

I wandered into the kitchen around eight or so, where Calvin brewed a pot of coffee for himself and Chloe...whenever she decided to emerge... while I settled for some cinnamon tea. Not for the first time, I reminded myself that I'd never been addicted to caffeine and that it was totally fine to be drinking something unleaded.

Right.

But at least I'd slept well and felt about as rested as I could, considering I couldn't change positions during the night the way I used to before I was carrying a ten-pound bowling ball around everywhere. And all right, Dr. Carlisle had said the baby would probably end up around seven or eight pounds, not the ten-plus I'd been fearing, considering how big Calvin and his brothers had been when they were born, but still, the extra weight got to you after a while no matter how hard you worked to compensate for it.

Chloe came in just as Calvin was pouring a cup of coffee for himself. For all I knew, she'd been asleep the whole time and had only roused herself now because the scent of the French roast had drifted down the hallway to the guest bedroom.

"That smells amazing," she said as he got a mug from the cupboard and filled it for her. She thanked him, then headed over to the fridge so she could add some milk to it.

"Sleep well?" I asked, and she nodded.

"Like a rock. It felt so much better to be out here and not alone at that Airbnb."

Maybe that was part of the problem. We hadn't talked much about her college experience, but it sounded to me as if she'd always lived at home and had never been alone at night. I had to admit that the first time I'd slept by myself in my new apartment after I moved out, I kept waking up all night, starting at every single sound. Soon enough I got used to knowing there wasn't anyone else around —well, except the people who lived in the neighboring apartments—but still, if it wasn't the sort of thing Chloe was used to, then her heebie-jeebies would have been understandable even if her boyfriend hadn't been murdered a few yards away from where she slept.

"That's good," I said, even as Calvin shot me a look from under his eyelashes. It seemed pretty clear to me that, while he was willing to indulge my whims and allow my sister to stay here for a day or two, he wanted me to know that this couldn't be a permanent situation.

And I had no intention of letting it turn into that. No, we'd give Chloe a day or two to clear her head, and then we'd be on the hunt for something more permanent. In fact, I'd already started to think it would be smarter to have Josie look for a house I could buy for my little sister, a place that could truly be her own. That way, she'd be more inclined to look at Globe as a real home, and not just someplace where she was hanging out for a while until she figured out what she wanted to do with the rest of her life.

She turned out to be fairly handy in the kitchen, too, whipping up some pancakes as fluffy as anything I could have made while I sat down at the table by the window and Calvin handled bacon duty. Soon enough, we were sitting in the dining room having breakfast, while the bright morning sun poured in and told me it was going to be another beautiful day.

So beautiful, in fact, that after breakfast Calvin excused himself to go work in the yard. He'd bought several bags of grass seed at the garden center the other day, and since the lovely weather looked as though it was going to continue, with no threat of frost overnight, he decided now was the time to get the new lawn going.

That left Chloe and me to our own devices. We both excused ourselves to go shower, then headed back into the living room some forty minutes or so later. I'd been thinking of the best way to broach the subject of buying a house rather than moving from Airbnb to Airbnb, and had even brought my laptop out to the living room so my sister and I could look over the listings together.

However, as soon as she sat down on the couch

and flipped her still-damp hair over her shoulders, my breath seemed to catch in my throat.

Hanging around her neck was a silver medallion with a design I hadn't seen for several years. It featured a moon on one side and a stylized tree on the other, stamped onto a round piece of sterling about an inch and a half wide.

The symbol for the Greater Los Angeles Necromancers' Guild.

Chapter 15

THE GLANG'S ALL HERE

Somehow, I managed to force out the words. "Where did you get that?"

Chloe's gaze strayed downward to the medallion revealed by the deep V of the long-sleeved T-shirt she was wearing. "This? Jack gave it to me. I guess it belonged to his aunt. It was with my jewelry when I was looking through it this morning, so I thought I might as well wear it as a sort of way of letting Jack know I was sorry about what happened."

"'Jack's aunt'?" I echoed. It was probably a good thing I was sitting down, or otherwise my suddenly shaky limbs might have betrayed me. "Who was his aunt?"

Looking mystified at my sudden interest in the heirloom she wore, Chloe replied, "Her name was

Athene Kappas. She was Jack's dad's younger sister. I guess she died a couple of years ago in a car crash."

I forced myself to take a breath, then another. Yes, Athene had died almost three years earlier, in a crash caused by a hex that Lucien Dumond's evil younger brother had placed on the car owned by Travis Cox, who was still Globe's one and only Uber/Lyft driver.

But....

If she had been Max Speros' younger sister—separated by a gap that must have been at least ten years or more—then why didn't they have the same name? True, I didn't know for an absolute fact that Athene had never been married, but she also never gave the impression that she'd been married and divorced, either.

All right. I needed to take this one step at a time.

Before I could formulate my next question, though, Chloe went on, "I guess she went by Kappas because that was Jack's grandmother's last name. Something about not wanting to perpetuate the oppression of the patriarchy."

Well, I had to admit that sounded like something Athene would say.

Gathering myself, I said, "Was Jack close to his aunt?"

"Not really," Chloe replied. "He didn't talk about her very much. He just said that she'd fought with his father years ago when Jack was in junior high and didn't have anything to do with the family after that."

Hmm. I couldn't pretend to know the exact timeline of Athene's involvement with Lucien and GLANG, but I'd gotten the impression that they'd been together for at least seven or eight years, maybe longer.

Had that long-ago quarrel stemmed from her decision to enter the world of the occult and join the guild?

If it had, that wouldn't surprise me very much. A lot of families had a difficult time accepting that their family members had chosen a different path from theirs.

"I guess the medallion was with Athene's stuff, and it all came to Jack's dad because she didn't have any other close family," Chloe said. "And his dad gave it to Jack, and Jack gave it to me because he thought it was pretty." She stopped there and gave me a probing look. "Why would it be important? It's just a pretty necklace, right?"

Oh, no, it was much more than that. I didn't think it was necessarily magical, but the medallion certainly represented a period in my life I would much rather have forgotten. As a member of L.A.'s psychic community, I'd been invited to Lucien's compound in Encino several times and had been unlucky enough to catch his eye. In fact, his unhealthy interest in me was the whole reason I'd fled Southern California in the first place.

"No," I said, then paused. While I really didn't want to go into the whole story, I knew I needed to tell Chloe why the medallion was important, and why it had a connection to me that she probably would never have guessed.

So I launched into the narrative as best I could, explaining what GLANG was, who had founded it —and how Jack's aunt Athene had been Lucien Dumond's right-hand woman, only to follow him in death during his brother Eugene's unholy quest to get his hands on Lucien's not-inconsiderable fortune...the same fortune that had come to me.

"You knew Jack's aunt?" Chloe breathed. "That's...wild."

Well, I supposed that was one word for it. "She was...an interesting person. And she definitely didn't deserve what happened to her."

Those words seemed to echo in my mind. They weren't so different from what I'd thought about poor Jack Speros's death only a few days earlier.

Jack Speros's death....

And then the cards flashed through my mind. The Devil...the Seven of Swords.

The Emperor.

Oh, dear Goddess.

"What is it?" Chloe asked then, brows drawing together in worry. "You're white as a sheet."

Of course I was. Because the terrible truth had awakened in me as I thought of the way Athene Kappas had been murdered, how someone had placed a hex on Travis's car...just as they'd placed a hex on mine.

Jack's murderer wasn't from Globe.

The Emperor card could also signify a father figure.

Jack's father, who'd been Athene's older brother.

No wonder I couldn't get Bryce Arsenault to neatly fit into the puzzle no matter how much I tried.

"Max Speros killed Jack," I whispered.

Chloe stared at me as though I'd lost my mind. In a way, I wished I had. It would have been easier than acknowledging that a father could do such a terrible thing to his son.

"Why would you say that?"

I rubbed my suddenly damp palms on the knees of my leggings, the only kind of pants my waistline would tolerate these days.

"You told me that Jack kept talking about getting married," I said, and Chloe nodded, expression still mystified.

"He did. But why would that make his father want to kill him?"

"Oh, I doubt he had murder on his mind at first," I replied. The image was becoming slowly clearer in my mind, buoyed by all the things the cards and the pendulum had already told me.

Temptation. Betrayal.

"I don't know exactly how," I went on. "But somehow, Max Speros must have discovered that the half-sister you'd never met was the same woman that Lucien Dumond had left all his money to. He must have wanted Jack to marry you so he could figure out a way to get me to give you some...or maybe all...of the money."

"That seems like a pretty crazy plan," Chloe said, now looking even more dubious.

"People do crazy things when millions of dollars are at stake," I replied.

She blinked. "That Lucien guy left you that much money?"

"Yes. And it's been earning interest ever since. Chloe...it's a lot."

My comment made her go quiet for a moment. When she spoke again, her voice trembled...and I couldn't really blame her.

"Is that why Jack asked me out in the first place? Because his father thought he could get to that money through me?"

My heart ached for her. And the horrible thing was, I couldn't say for sure. Not without a whole lot more facts in hand than I currently had.

"I don't know," I said gently. "It's possible that

Max Speros only learned of the connection after you'd been with Jack for a while."

She didn't reply at first, maybe because she was trying out the different scenarios in her mind and trying to decide which one seemed more plausible. "But why would Mr. Speros even think he was entitled to that money?"

At least there we were on slightly more neutral ground. "Probably because he would have known that Athene was Lucien's lieutenant, for lack of a better word. It would only have made sense that Lucien's money would have gone to her upon his death, since I knew he didn't want to leave it to his family, and of course he couldn't have known that she would die shortly after he did. Because Lucien didn't know who he could trust, he left the money to me instead."

Mostly on a whim, because Lucien Dumond, a double Scorpio who'd definitely lived up to the destiny the stars had dictated to him, had a twisted sense of humor. It amused him to make the woman who'd fled the state rather than succumb to his dubious charms the beneficiary of his vast estate, rather than leave it to the parents who'd raised his murderous brother...or to the followers who had often renounced their own families rather than abandon GLANG.

Just like Athene, apparently.

"I still don't understand why Mr. Speros would

kill Jack," Chloe said. Now she sounded almost plaintive, as if her mind didn't want to accept the horrible truth that the man who'd acted as though he wanted to accept her into his family could do such an awful thing. "I mean, we were broken up. There wasn't anything else he could have done to keep us together."

But I knew that individuals in pursuit of millions of dollars didn't give up so easily. However, we were talking about people who'd been in her life for several years, people she didn't want to believe could be capable of such terrible things.

"Maybe not at first look," I said. "But why do you think Jack was here in Globe that night?"

Chloe stared back at me, dawning comprehension in her face. "Because his father made him come here to try to get me back?"

"That seems the most plausible explanation."

She shook her head then, confusion returning to her expression. "But why would he have killed Jack if he was doing what his father told him to do?"

A very good question. It seemed to me that we'd reached the point where we couldn't waste any more time on speculation.

No, we needed to get to the heart of the matter. "Are Jack's parents still here in Globe?"

"I—I don't know for sure," Chloe replied.

Then, as comprehension appeared to sink in, she added in worried tones, “You’re not actually going to try to *talk* to them, are you?”

“Of course,” I said. “That’s the only way to get to the bottom of this. But don’t worry,” I went on, knowing I needed to say something to allay her fears, “We’re going to have backup.”

Obviously, I wasn’t crazy enough to confront the Speroses on my own, although I’d performed similar feats of foolhardiness in the past. Now, though, I had the baby’s safety to worry about as well as my own, and I figured there weren’t a lot of things more intimidating than my six-foot-six police chief husband.

He’d listened to the appalling story with a deepening frown, and then reluctantly agreed to go to the Airbnb where Jack’s parents were staying.

“But I’ve got Henry’s number locked and loaded,” Calvin added, touching the pocket where he kept his cell phone.

That was fine by me. I didn’t have any qualms about calling in the cavalry if things turned nasty. Besides, Globe wasn’t my husband’s jurisdiction, and if Max and Leslie Speros ended up spilling the beans about their son’s murder, then the local police would have to be the ones to make the arrest.

"You're staying here, though," I told Chloe, and at once her slate-colored eyes flashed with rebellious fire.

"I have a right to hear what they have to say," she said. "Jack was my boyfriend, you know."

"Ex-boyfriend," I reminded her gently, and she seemed to deflate a little.

"Okay, fine," she said. "But still, I deserve to know what really happened to him. And don't try telling me it isn't safe, because if you're willing to go in there when you're about to pop at any second, I don't want to hear it."

A quick glance at my husband told me he was doing his best to hold back a smile.

And Chloe had a point.

"All right," I said. "But you'll let Calvin and me do most of the talking...and you'll have your phone in hand, ready to call 9-1-1, just in case."

This must have seemed a simple enough accommodation to make, because she didn't try to argue but only nodded.

"I'm good with that."

There didn't seem to be much point in delaying...especially since it was now inching toward eleven, which I knew was the check-out time for Mavis's Airbnbs. Quite possibly, Max and Leslie had already left to make the long drive back to Southern California, and we'd have to figure out some other way to confront them with my suspicions.

Exactly how, I had no idea. There was no way I could travel to L.A. in my condition, and this wasn't exactly the sort of meeting that would have the same impact if conducted via Zoom.

None of us said much on the drive over to their vacation rental. My mind kept playing with scenarios, trying to figure out which one would be worse...to find them already gone, or to have to face them after all.

Calvin pulled up to the curb in front of the Airbnb and parked. At once, Chloe opened her door and got out, but I waited for my husband to come around and help me down from the passenger seat. Not for the first time, I reflected how good it would feel to have this over with, to not feel as if my body was completely alien to me. Yes, all the baby books I'd read had said it would still feel forever altered once I'd given birth, but still, at least I wouldn't have to worry about toppling over like a bowling pin at an inopportune moment.

With Calvin's hand in mine and Chloe tagging along only a foot or so behind, we made our way to the front door. He knocked, and I almost held my breath, wondering whether anyone was going to answer it after all.

But then Leslie Speros opened the door, and

almost at once, her eyes widened in surprise as she took in the three of us standing outside on the porch.

However, her tone wasn't quite as hostile as I'd been fearing. "Can I help you with something? We were just about to leave."

"I'm sorry to catch you at the last minute like this," I said. "But there was something Chloe and I needed to talk to you about."

One of Leslie's brows lifted, and I couldn't help noticing the way she glanced over at Calvin, as if trying to figure out why he was there if this was a matter that only involved my sister and me.

"My car's in the shop, so Calvin offered to drive," I said.

It seemed that explanation was enough to convince her, because she stepped out of the way and let us inside. However, I noticed how her hand shook as she reached out to close the door, and I had a feeling she wasn't quite as casual as she wanted the rest of us to believe.

Several weekender bags sat near the couch, so it seemed she'd been telling the truth when she'd informed us that she and her husband were about to head back to California. In fact, Max Speros came into the living room right then, a frown creasing his forehead as he took in his unexpected visitors.

But, like his wife, he sounded cordial enough as

he said, "Good morning. Is there something we can help you with?"

"Selena said she and Chloe had something they needed to talk to us about."

Max's gaze flicked over to my sister and then back to me. "Oh?"

This was going to be a lot harder than I'd thought, especially with how normal they were both acting. Was it possible that I'd made a hideous mistake and that they were both perfectly innocent?

But then Max's aura emerged, like a monsoon thundercloud welling up from the dry desert floor, grayish black, shot through with yellowish bursts like foul lightning.

That wasn't the aura of an innocent man.

No, I thought as my stomach twisted in disgust, it was one that revealed how truly evil he was.

"I know you killed your son," I said clearly, and Leslie's hand went to her mouth.

Something about the gesture was a little too practiced, though, a little too theatrical. In that moment—especially when her own bruised aura emerged for a split second, only to disappear again —I knew she was just as guilty as her husband.

Of course. The Queen of Cups, reversed. Co-dependency, weakness.

She'd wanted that money, too...enough that

she was just fine with emotional blackmail and even murder to get it.

"That's ridiculous," Max Speros said, his tone cold enough to drop the temperature in the room by at least ten degrees. "And utterly insulting."

"No, it's true," Chloe chimed in. "Selena told me about Lucien Dumond's money and your sister Athene. It makes total sense—you thought you could get to Selena's inheritance by going through me. I guess my question is, did you encourage Jack to date me, or was it just a stroke of luck that your son started seeing the half-sister of the woman who inherited the money you thought you were entitled to?"

For a long moment, neither Max nor Leslie said anything, and I wondered what I would do if they tried to stonewall us. I supposed I had enough evidence that I could go to Henry Lewis and hope he'd think it was sufficient to place them both under arrest, but I couldn't be sure of that.

Then Max Speros' mouth quirked in a lopsided smile. There was absolutely no humor in his expression, though, and I wondered if the smile had turned out so crooked because he couldn't quite get all his facial muscles to obey.

"I think you need to leave," he said, but Calvin stepped forward, expression utterly blank.

When he looked like that, anyone who knew him well also knew they shouldn't fool around.

"Chloe asked you a question."

That was all he said, but I saw the way his hand rested on his hip—the same hip where he was wearing his service revolver. I'd never once seen him fire it, but that didn't mean he wouldn't...in the right situation.

And although I was halfway worried that Max would still challenge him, would say this wasn't his jurisdiction and he needed to butt out, it seemed Jack's father was a little fuzzy on that aspect of the situation. He forced a chuckle that didn't fool any of us, then said, "I don't have to say anything without a lawyer present."

"You're not under arrest, Mr. Speros," Calvin replied. "The Miranda laws don't apply."

"Maybe not," Leslie put in, her face white with strain, "but that also doesn't mean we have to stand here and listen to these sorts of horrible accusations."

Stalemate. I allowed myself the smallest of glances toward my husband, but his attention was fixed on the Speroses, not me.

But then Chloe stepped forward, chin up. "You made him date me," she said, her voice firm, dark gray eyes blazing with fury. "You made him do whatever he had to so we'd stay together. And then when we broke up, you wouldn't let him walk away. What happened that night, Mr. Speros? Did Jack finally grow a spine, and you strangled him because you realized he wasn't any use to you and he might tell me the truth about what was really going on?"

No response...except maybe the smallest twitch of one of the muscles near Max's left eye.

But that was enough for me.

And yet I still wanted to know for sure.

"How did Jack get in Chloe's Airbnb?" I pressed, ignoring Max Speros' continuing silence. "There wasn't any sign of forced entry. Did one of you pick the lock?"

Now a flicker of contempt showed in his dark eyes. "No need for that. Or did you think that my sister Athene was the only one in our family with any magical ability?"

Of course. He'd used some kind of charm to open the lock...just as he'd probably placed that hex on my car. I couldn't know for sure whether he'd been trying to kill me or simply move me off the chessboard so I wouldn't continue trying to track down his son's killer. And when that gambit had failed, he and his wife had decided the best thing to do was to get the heck out of Dodge and do everything they could to make sure suspicion never fell on them.

Not that their plans really mattered at his point.

He raised his hands—to do what, I wasn't sure,

since I didn't practice the kind of dark magic utilized by practitioners of the black arts.

Chloe made a move forward. To protect me against the coming blast?

I didn't have a chance to find out, because at the same moment, Calvin's gun went off, impossibly loud in the confined space.

A bright red stain appeared on the knee of Max Speros's jeans, and he let out a cry of pain, whatever spell he'd been intending to cast forgotten as he fell to the floor. His wife uttered a shocked sound as well and dropped to her knees next to him.

Grim-faced, Calvin holstered his gun and then unclipped the handcuffs he'd had hanging from his belt. "Max Speros, I'm placing you under arrest for the murder of your son, Jack Speros."

The room seemed to spin around me. I wondered if the sudden dizziness was just the aftermath of hearing the pistol go off in the small room, but then an odd wetness soaked my leggings, making me look down in sudden comprehension.

"Good timing," I said.

"Because I think my water just broke."

Chapter 16

FAMILY TIES

"SELENA, I REALLY NEED TO GET YOUR statement," Henry Lewis told me, his tone urgent.

"Nine centimeters dilation," said the nurse at the bottom of my bed.

"Henry, I'm kind of in the middle of something!" I snapped. Good thing the table in my hospital room that currently held a bedpan was too far for me to reach, or I probably would have grabbed it and hurled it at his head.

Calvin's fingers tightened on mine. He hadn't left my side for a single second, not even in the chaotic aftermath of his blowing out Max Speros's kneecap and calling the Globe P.D. to the scene... right after he'd contacted 9-1-1 to come and take me to the hospital. The police and the ambulance had shown up around the same time, so while I saw Henry come marching toward the house with several of his deputies in tow, I'd already been loaded onto a gurney and wheeled down the front walk of the Airbnb where Jack's parents had been staying.

That was probably why the police chief had hurried over to the hospital to get all the details from Calvin and me. Although Henry knew my husband would never discharge his service pistol without a damn good reason, he still needed to hear the details of the confrontation from both of us.

Unfortunately, I was a little occupied at the moment. For whatever reason, this baby had decided it was time to make his or her appearance today. Things had moved so fast that the OB-GYN on duty at the medical center hadn't even been able to give me an epidural, which hadn't improved my mood very much.

Another contraction wracked my body, and I gripped the sheets, grimacing as I held back a shriek of pain. The last thing I wanted was to be screaming like a crazy woman in front of Henry Lewis, even though his wife had been through this twice herself and he probably had a good idea of the level of stress I was dealing with right now.

"You don't need her statement," Calvin said. He still sounded remarkably calm, all things considered, but somewhere outside my pain, I thought I detected a distinct edge to his voice. "I already told you what happened. Max Speros lunged for Selena, obviously meaning her bodily harm, and I had no choice but to neutralize him. Your time would be better spent interrogating the Speroses—I have a feeling Leslie is the weak link. You just need to put a little pressure on her."

Henry's eyes narrowed. However, he seemed to realize this wasn't the time to let Calvin know he shouldn't be telling him how to do his job, because he gave us both a curt nod and then said, "I'll get out of your hair. But I may have more questions later."

"Great," I gritted. "You know where to find us."

He left then, and Calvin's grasp on my hand tightened a little. It didn't hurt, though. No, that firm grip on my fingers told me he was going to be there through everything.

Not that I'd doubted him for a second.

Dr. Carlisle came in then, smiling. "Well, Selena, it looks like it's time. This one's definitely ready to come into the world."

I sent her an apologetic look. "Sorry we're early —and for dragging you here on a Sunday."

Her smile only widened. "Kind of comes with the territory. Babies don't have much use for schedules. Calvin, we're going to need you to get suited up—I assume you want to be there for the birth."

"Of course," he replied, then leaned down to

press a kiss against my forehead. "You're doing great, Selena."

I supposed I was. Or at least, it seemed all my worries about being in labor for thirty-six hours or some other ungodly span of time had been for nothing. Barely an hour had elapsed since the ambulance picked me up at the Airbnb, and already the contractions were only a few minutes apart. And yes, they hurt, worse than anything else I'd ever experienced, but knowing this was all going to be over soon made me able to hang on.

The nurses wheeled my hospital bed down the corridor to the delivery room. Calvin stayed beside me the whole way, although he had to pause before he could enter so he could put on some scrubs. Several more nurses were waiting for us, and soon enough they helped me onto the delivery table.

This was real. I was going to have a baby.

Another contraction spasmed through my body, and instinctively, I started to push. Anything to get this over with.

"Not yet, Selena," Dr. Carlisle told me. "I need you to breathe. Can you do that for me?"

About all I could do was nod.

Not big gulps of air, though.

Rhythmic pants, just the way they'd taught Calvin and me in Lamaze class. He was there then, jeans and shirt covered up by aqua-green scrubs.

"Perfect," he said, his voice soothing. "You're amazing."

"So—are—you," I panted. It was the best thing in the world to have him with me right then. I honestly couldn't understand how some women would scream at their husbands or significant others about getting them in this mess at such a moment, not when I knew this would have been so much more difficult if I'd been going through such an ordeal without him at my side.

He smiled.

"All right," Dr. Carlisle said. "Time to push. Are you ready?"

Was I? The moment that baby came into the world, everything would change.

Unfortunately, I didn't have much say in the matter.

A contraction wracked my body, but I managed to nod, breathing in and out, pushing... pushing hard.

And then I was spent and had to stop so I could pull in more air.

"That was great," Dr. Carlisle told me. "Another one, and I think we'll be there."

Just another push. I thought I could do that.

Calvin bent down and pressed a kiss against my forehead. "You can do this."

Yes, I could...and I would.

A groan tore its way out of my throat as I bore

down again, and this time, I could feel something give way, could feel the weight that had been pressing against my pelvis for the past six months finally ease.

And then a sharp cry filled the room.

"Wonderful," Dr. Carlisle said as a nurse rushed over with a towel to pick up the baby and wrap the round little body securely. "Selena, Calvin...I'd like to introduce you to your new daughter."

Happy tears trailed down my cheeks as the nurse came over with my daughter and laid her in my arms. Calvin bent down, marveling at the tiny, tiny fingers and toes, the lush fringe of black lashes that lay against her red cheeks.

"She's perfect," he said, and kissed me again. "Just like her mother."

What could I do except smile?

"That is probably the prettiest baby I've ever seen," Josie declared as she gazed down into the bassinet. "Just don't tell Terry and Brett that. I love my niece and nephews, but I have to say they didn't look this good when they came into the world."

I allowed myself a grin. "Your secret is safe with me."

Because the birth had been so uneventful, I was

allowed to go home the next day. And while some people might have waited a while to have visitors, two days after that, I felt well enough to have my friends and family over to see baby Celeste.

Possibly I was biased, but I had to admit she was a gorgeous little thing, with those long, long lashes and thick dark hair. Her eyes looked as though they were going to stay blue, which surprised me a little. I would have thought Calvin's genetic contribution would have made sure she was as dark-eyed as he was.

We'd just have to wait and see on that, though.

"She's a good baby, too," I said. "She's only been waking me up two or three times a night, so I count that as a win."

"Well, I hope she's waking up Calvin, too," Josie said, now looking a little stern.

"Obviously," I replied. "And he's a champ at diaper duty. But that's probably because he's had so much practice with his nieces and nephews."

Josie nodded at that comment, then said, "I'm just glad your mother took Chloe in, since this all happened so last minute."

That was for sure. I'd told my sister that I'd find her another Airbnb to stay in, but obviously, nature had intervened. But my mother stepped up and said they had plenty of room at the old Bigelow mansion, and Chloe had taken her up on the offer.

Maybe some people would have found the setup a little odd. I just looked at the arrangement as my family coming together, the way they were supposed to.

"She and my mom are coming by in a little while," I said. "Did you want to stay and say hi?"

Josie looked regretful. "I wish I could, but I have a house showing after this. I just wanted to pop in and see the baby...and see how you were doing, of course."

I was fine. More than fine, really, and I thought everyone could see that.

A few minutes later, Josie left, promising she would stop by again in a few days.

And then my mother and Chloe came over, ostensibly to check in to see whether I was still chugging along, but really so they could spend some time with the baby. I was a little surprised by how well my sister had adapted to being an aunt, and as for my mother, well, she was over the moon to hold her first grandchild and give me some much-needed free time for a hot bath or anything else I might need.

But as wrapped up as I was in reveling in being a new mother—and, with Calvin, experiencing every little sigh and coo and bubble like the new miracle it was—I'd managed to get the lowdown on what was happening with Max and Leslie Speros.

Apparently, once Henry talked to them separately, Leslie had broken down and confessed everything, saying she'd gone along with her husband's wishes because they needed the money—they had two mortgages on their house and multiple maxed-out credit cards, and couldn't see a way out of the mess they were in. Of course, she also said she had no idea that her husband planned to kill their son, only that he'd followed him to Globe to make sure he patched up his relationship with Chloe any way he possibly could so they could use her as a means of getting at my inherited fortune. The "garrote" had been a clay cutter Max had gotten from their garage, a relic of their daughter Emma's one semester of taking pottery in high school, something he'd grabbed at the last minute after he realized that throttling his son with his bare hands probably wasn't a very good idea.

Despite Leslie's protestations of innocence, she'd been charged as an accessory to murder, and both of them were in jail awaiting trial. It seemed the judge didn't trust them to honor their bail, not when they were so in debt and the Mexican border was only a hundred miles or so away.

That didn't mean there weren't some niggling questions that needed to be cleared up.

"I still don't understand how Jack tracked me here to Globe, though," Chloe told me the day after Josie's visit. Little Celeste was sleeping in her bassinet, and my sister and I sat in the living room with the windows open, glad of another unseasonably mild day, a promise of warmer weather soon to come.

I'd been thinking about Jack's appearance in Globe quite a bit—well, in between being obsessed with the new baby—and an idea had occurred to me. "I think it was Athene's medallion," I said, and Chloe's eyes went wide. "I think Max Speros placed some kind of tracking charm on it, then put the idea in Jack's head to give it to you. That way, he'd always know where you were."

"That's creepy," she said, her tone emphatic, and I nodded.

"Extremely creepy. But it's obvious he was a very controlling parent. Was he like that with Jack's brother and sister?"

Chloe reached up to push a lock of dark hair back over her shoulder. "Not that I really noticed. But then, his older brother Ethan had already graduated from Stanford and had decided to stay in the Bay Area, so I didn't see him very much. And Jack's little sister Emma was so busy with cheerleading and all her other activities that she also wasn't around a lot of the time."

What would those two do now, with both their parents in jail and very likely facing substantial amounts of prison time? Maybe Ethan was old enough to manage on his own, but Emma....

I asked Chloe about that, and her expression grew sympathetic.

"Jack's Aunt Tracy—his mom's sister—was pretty close to the family, so I think Emma would probably go live with her."

That was good to hear. All the same, I made a mental note to set up some kind of fund for Emma, enough to get her through college and have a decent start on life.

After all, none of this was her fault.

Chloe didn't stay very long, as she'd only popped over during an extended lunch break. But I could see from the lightness of her step that, while she might have mourned Jack and his terrible end, she was ready to move on. As far as I was able to tell, my mother loved having her at the house, so there wasn't any rush to find her a permanent place to live.

Eventually, though, she'd need a home of her own, and I did not doubt that Josie would help us find it when the time came.

And Calvin, although on leave from his job as chief of the San Ramon police for the next six weeks, was keeping in contact with his deputies... especially Ben Ironhorse, the one with the computer-hacking skills.

"Turns out that Max Speros was also involved with GLANG when it first started up," Calvin told me. We sat together on the couch, a sleeping

Celeste cradled in his arms. She'd just had her afternoon feeding and was now zonked out, little spit bubbles forming on her Cupid's bow lips. "But it sounds like he had a falling out with Lucien, and that was when Athene stepped in. This would have been long before you ran afoul of Dumond."

"How did Ben find all that out?" I asked, and Calvin only smiled.

"Trade secret."

I stuck my tongue out at my husband and he laughed, even as he leaned over to press a kiss against my cheek—but gently, so he wouldn't wake up our daughter.

However, that additional piece of information helped fill in more of the puzzle. Max had been playing with dark magic for a long time, which explained why he'd been able to put the tracking charm on Athene's medallion and that awful hex on my Jeep. Exactly what had passed between father and son on that awful night we might never know—well, at least until the trial—but clearly, they'd argued, and Max had decided to rid himself of a son he now viewed as a liability.

After all, he had two other children.

Or at least, that was how I guessed his thought processes might have gone. How any parent could murder their own child, I had no idea, but as much as I hated to admit it, this wasn't the first time that awful scenario had played out…and I knew it wouldn't be the last.

"Love you both," I said fiercely, and Calvin's dark eyes met mine.

A nod, as if he understood where that comment had come from. "Love you both," he said softly. "Now and forever."

I leaned my head against his shoulder. Thank the Goddess for Calvin, and for all the love he'd given me over the past few years. Because of him, I knew men such as Max Speros were an aberration. There were far more good people than evil in the world…if you only knew where to look.

On Thursday, Archie finally made it over to see the new arrival. Hazel and Chuck and Victoria had already visited several times, but Archie had seemed to come up with one excuse after another for not coming out to the house.

Was he worried that seeing a real live baby in action might make him reconsider his decision to start a family with Victoria?

If that was the case, it was a little too late to have him change his mind.

When he arrived, I was in the nursery, with Celeste freshly fed and down for another nap. He paused at the doorway, a stuffed pink teddy bear in one hand and an almost sheepish expression on his face.

Well, sheepish for Archie, anyway.

"Sorry I couldn't come sooner," he said, his gaze not quite meeting mine. "Things have been busy at the studio with the floor refinishing and everything."

Yes, I vaguely remembered him saying that they were going to sand everything down and put on a fresh coat of urethane, a housekeeping chore that needed to happen every year or so because of all the wear and tear the studio floors suffered during those weekly dance classes.

"It's fine," I assured him, and it was. While I appreciated all the visits—and all the praise for Celeste—I also thought it wasn't a bad idea to space things out a bit. "And the teddy bear is adorable."

I went over to him and he handed me the bear, which I set down on the easy chair in the corner. I'd need to move it before Celeste's next feeding, but that shouldn't be for a while.

"You look well," Archie observed. "Thinner."

About all I could do was chuckle. "Well, I dropped over ten pounds this week."

True, Celeste had weighed in at seven pounds, eleven ounces, but the rest of it was my body beginning to shed some of the other weight that had come along with the pregnancy. Calvin and I had both agreed that I wouldn't worry about trying to get back to my usual size six any time soon, and yet it seemed my metabolism had its own opinion on the matter.

Archie nodded, then went over to the bassinet so he could look down at the sleeping infant inside. "She has a lot of hair," he observed, making the comment sound almost like a criticism.

"So do her parents," I replied with a smile. Again, only true. Calvin's hair was much longer than mine, but we both had thick, straight locks.

Another nod, this one almost distracted. Then Archie turned back toward me, clear blue eyes almost pleading. "Is it...is it hard?"

We'd known each other too long for me to do anything except answer truthfully. "Yes," I said. "It's hard. But it's also the best thing you'll ever do."

A corner of his mouth quirked. "Is that more of your fortune-telling?"

"Not at all," I replied. "It's just knowing. And I know you and Victoria will be wonderful parents. We'll all be here to support each other while we learn along the way."

He watched me for a moment, still with that half-worried flicker in his eyes, and then he inclined his head just the slightest bit. "You're a good friend, Selena."

"So are you, Archie. The best."

A hug so quick I almost didn't realize it was happening until he'd already let go of me, and then he murmured, "I need to get back to the studio."

I didn't say anything to stop him, but only smiled.

After checking on Celeste—who showed every sign of staying asleep for at least the next hour—I wandered into my office and paused there for a moment, gaze moving over the shelves of books and Tarot cards and crystals. I hadn't been in here very much this past week, for obvious reasons.

I'd had much more important things to occupy my time.

But then a hint of movement caught my eye, and I watched as pale mist swirled in the crystal ball on its shelf. At once, I picked it up, and carried it and its stand over to the altar.

A moment later, Grandma Ellen smiled at me from within the crystal ball.

"Congratulations," she said.

"Thank you," I replied. It touched me that she'd appeared like this, unbidden, rather than waiting for me to reach out to her. Before now, I'd always been the one to make contact.

"She's a beautiful girl," my grandmother went on. "And thank you for the name."

Because that was my daughter's full name—Celeste Ellen Standingbear. Calvin and I had gone back and forth on whether she should be a hyphenate, with my husband insisting that our daughter should carry both our names. Luckily, I'd managed to convince him that was an awfully big mouthful for such a little girl, and he'd relented.

But he'd been fully on board with giving her the middle name of the great-grandmother she'd never get to meet.

Well, unless Celeste ended up inheriting my psychic gifts and decided to use the crystal ball for advice from her ancestor, just as I had all these years.

"Calvin and I both wanted to honor you," I said.

Were those tears glittering in my grandmother's deep blue eyes, so similar to my own?

"It means more than I can say," she replied. "And I'm so glad to see you happy here with your new family and all your friends. And now that's what you'll be able to truly focus on."

Those words made me lift an eyebrow. "Are you saying I won't have any more murders to solve?"

She didn't answer for a moment, her gaze far away, as if fixed on something only she could see. "You've done the work you came here to do. Now is the time for a new stage in your life. I'm not saying you won't have plenty of opportunities to do good in your community, only that it might take a different form from what you've been doing these past few years. Many blessings to you, Selena."

The image in the crystal ball faded away then, but I had no desire to call my grandmother back. She'd reached out from the afterlife to send us all her love, and I couldn't ask for anything more than that.

Very gently, I picked up the crystal ball and its mount, then set them back in their usual spot on the bookshelf. Quite possibly, I wouldn't need them again...at least, not for a very long time.

But that was all right. My days would be filled with watching Celeste grow and become her own unique person, and eventually, I would go back to Once in a Blue Moon...or possibly not, depending on how things worked out. I knew the store would be just fine with Chloe at the helm, so maybe that part of my life was also over, with something new and exciting just around the corner.

I couldn't wait to find out what happened next.

This concludes the Hedgewitch for Hire series. For more books from Christine Pope, just turn the page!

Also by Christine Pope

THE DJINN WARS

(Paranormal Romance)

Chosen

Taken

Fallen

Broken

Forsaken

Forbidden

Awoken

Illuminated

Stolen

Forgotten

Driven

Unspoken

Hidden

Written

Given

Mistaken (October 2024)

FAMILIAR SPIRITS

(Cozy Mystery/Paranormal Romance)

Spells and Spaniels

Cauldrons and Cats

Hexes and Hedgehogs

Charms and Chihuahuas

Runes and Ravens

LATTES AND LEVITATION*

(Cozy Mystery/Paranormal Romance)

Caffeine Before Curses

Muffins After Magic

Pastries and Prophecies

Eclairs and Ectoplasm

Sugar Skulls and Specters

Wedding Cakes and Wishes

HEDGEWITCH FOR HIRE*

(Cozy Mystery/Paranormal Romance)

Grave Mistake

Social Medium

Household Demons

Perpetual Potion

Jingle Spells

Wandering Monsters

Uninvited Ghosts

Prophet Motive

Ballroom Bits

Spell Check

Brew Confessions

Charm School

UNEXPECTED MAGIC*

(Urban Fantasy/Paranormal Romance)

Found Objects

Finders, Keepers

Lost and Found

Finding Destiny

THE WITCHES OF WHEELER PARK*

(Paranormal Romance)

Storm Born

Thunder Road

Winds of Change

Mind Games

A Wheeler Park Christmas

Blood Ties

Healing Hands

Wishful Thinking

Smoke and Mirrors

MISS PRIMM'S ACADEMY FOR WAYWARD WITCHES*

(Fantasy/Academy Romance)

Misspelled

Dispelled

Expelled

PROJECT DEMON HUNTERS*

(Paranormal Romance)

Unquiet Souls

Unbound Spirits

Unholy Ground

Unseen Voices

Unmarked Graves

Unbroken Vows

THE DEVIL YOU KNOW*

(Paranormal Romance)

Sympathy for the Devil

Charmed, I'm Sure

A Wing and a Prayer

Wish Upon a Star

THE WITCHES OF CANYON ROAD*

(Paranormal Romance)

Hidden Gifts

Darker Paths

Mysterious Ways

A Canyon Road Christmas

Demon Born

An Ill Wind

Higher Ground

Haunted Hearts

THE WITCHES OF CLEOPATRA HILL*

(Paranormal Romance)

Darkangel

Darknight

Darkmoon

Sympathetic Magic

Protector

Spellbound

A Cleopatra Hill Christmas

Impractical Magic

Strange Magic

The Arrangement

Defender

Bad Blood

Deep Magic

Darktide

THE WATCHERS TRILOGY*

(Paranormal Romance)

Falling Dark

Dead of Night

Rising Dawn

THE SEDONA FILES*

(Paranormal/Science Fiction Romance)

Bad Vibrations

Desert Hearts

Angel Fire

Star Crossed

Falling Angels

Enemy Mine

TALES OF THE LATTER KINGDOMS*

(Fantasy Romance)

All Fall Down

Dragon Rose

Binding Spell

Ashes of Roses

One Thousand Nights

Threads of Gold

The Wolf of Harrow Hall

Moon Dance

The Song of the Thrush

THE GAIAN CONSORTIUM SERIES*

(Science Fiction Romance)

Beast (free prequel novella)

Blood Will Tell

Breath of Life

The Gaia Gambit

The Mandala Maneuver

The Titan Trap

The Zhore Deception

The Refugee Ruse

STANDALONE TITLES

Hearts on Fire (Paranormal Romance)

Taking Dictation (Contemporary Romance)

Golden Heart (Gaslamp Fantasy Romance)

Night Music: A Modern Reimagining of The Phantom of the Opera (Contemporary Romance)

Ghost Dance: A Sequel to Gaston Leroux's The Phantom of the Opera (Historical Mystery/Romance)

Flight Before Christmas (Fantasy Romance)

* Indicates a completed series

About the Author

USA Today bestselling author Christine Pope has been writing stories ever since she commandeered her family's Smith-Corona typewriter back in grade school. Her work includes paranormal romance, cozy paranormal mystery, and urban fantasy, among others. She makes her home in Arizona.

Christine Pope on the Web:
www.christinepope.com

facebook.com/ChristinePopeAuthor
pinterest.com/ChristineJPope
bookbub.com/authors/christine-pope

www.ingramcontent.com/pod-product-compliance
Lightning Source LLC
LaVergne TN
LVHW091106080826
845145LV00008B/1830

9781946435750